A QUESTION OF GUILT

Dane Spilwell, a brilliant surgeon, stands accused of the brutal murder of his wife. The evidence against him is damning, his guilt almost a foregone conclusion. Two red-haired women will determine his ultimate fate. One, a mysterious lady in emeralds, may be the key to clearing him of the crime — if only she can be located. The other, Detective Jilly Garvey, began by doggedly working to convict him — but now finds herself doubting his culpability . . .

Books by Tony Gleeson
in the Linford Mystery Library:

NIGHT MUSIC
IT'S HER FAULT

TONY GLEESON

A QUESTION OF GUILT

Complete and Unabridged

LINFORD
Leicester

First published in Great Britain

First Linford Edition
published 2016

Copyright © 2015 by Tony Gleeson

A catalogue record for this book is available
from the British Library.

ISBN 978–1–4448–2915–0

Published by
F. A. Thorpe (Publishing)
Anstey, Leicestershire

Set by Words & Graphics Ltd.
Anstey, Leicestershire
Printed and bound in Great Britain by
T. J. International Ltd., Padstow, Cornwall

This book is printed on acid-free paper

Dedication:
To Jack, who will know why

1

One year later, Jilly Garvey would still recall that September night vividly. She and Reggie Martinez walked from the dark of the murky alley into the glare of artificial light, into the small crowd busily milling around the trash dumpster. They showed their identification to one of the officers, who nodded them through, past the yellow tape that had already been strung. One of the medical examiners rose from one knee to greet them.

'Detectives, lovely night.'

They had already decided it was Reggie's turn to take the lead on this one. He nodded to the ME. 'Isn't it always, Joshua. So what have we got here?'

'She was found behind the bin there. Stabbed several times.' He gestured to the body splayed out on the ground. Camera flashes went off in rapid succession around them.

'Who found the body?'

Joshua pointed to the other end of the alley to a slight, frightened-looking young man: thick, unruly mop of hair; dark shapeless overcoat over a white apron and dark pants. He stood between two uniformed officers.

'Works in a restaurant around the corner. They dump a lot of stuff in here on Wednesday evenings. Apparently he was dropping stuff into the hopper and saw the body. Called it in on his cell.'

'I'll go talk to him,' said Jilly, exchanging nods with Reggie.

Crime techs were busily at work all around and she walked carefully, making sure to avoid the places they were processing. She held up her ID to the uniforms, and they nodded and stepped away from the guy, who looked even more frightened now.

'I'm Detective Garvey,' she said, trying to sound non-threatening. 'You're the person who found her?'

The guy just nodded, eyeing her carefully.

'Don't worry, you're not in any trouble.

I just need to ask you some questions, okay?'

'They already did that,' the guy replied in a hoarse voice, nodding his head back and forth to the two uniforms.

'Well, I have to ask some more, okay? What's your name?'

'Bertie,' he said, uneasily.

'Okay, Bertie. Got a last name? It's okay, really.'

Bertie waited a beat before quietly saying, 'Grossman.'

'Okay, Bertie. So tell me what happened.'

'I'm a busboy at Monica's, out on the main street. I was dumping a bunch of food into the dumpster, and I saw something back there, behind it.' He pointed with a quivering finger. 'I could see the blood. I could see her face. Her eyes were wide open!'

'Is it normal for you to be out here dumping food?'

'Oh yeah, the restaurant makes us do it a couple times a week. Kind of a waste, a lot of it is still good, we could be giving it to poor folks or something, you know? In

3

no time there'll be homeless people back here 'cause the word is out that we do that.'

'Okay, I get it, Bertie. So you saw her and what'd you do?'

'I kinda . . . freaked out for a minute, you know? Never seen somebody dead like that.'

'Uh-huh. So then what'd you do?'

'I was going to run back to the restaurant, but then I decided to call 911 from right here.'

'Did you go back to the restaurant after that?'

'Yeah, I told the manager what had happened. I was totally freaked out, you know? She told me, calm down and go back out and wait for the cops. I couldn't bring myself to come back here, so I waited out there.' He pointed to the mouth of the alleyway.

'Did anybody else from the restaurant come back here?'

'No, I think Lavonne, she's the manager, kept it to herself.'

'Smart lady. Didn't want to start a fuss.' She asked a few more questions about the restaurant and the manager, got contact information for Bertie, tried again to reassure him and thank him for his help.

Then she returned to Reggie, who was talking with another of the uniforms and busily jotting in his notebook. They were standing over the body. The MEs moved aside to let her have a look.

She walked around it, looking carefully, crouching to inspect aspects at closer detail. The woman was on her back, arms and legs spread, elbows bent. A pair of stylish tinted eyeglasses lay at an odd tilt on her face. An expensive-looking long coat splayed open; underneath, she wore a beige dress with numerous red blotches that had spread from her wounds.

'Whatcha think, Red?' Reggie asked, still writing furiously. His pet name for his partner, referring to the natural color of her hair. 'Reg and Red', they were called at the station.

'Several stabs. Looks like they were delivered hard and fast. Angry assailant?'

'Very possibly.'

'Nice clothes. Coat's cashmere. Dress

looks like real silk. Nice jewelry. Nails carefully done, nice haircut. I'd guess designer eyewear. She's hardly low rent.'

Reggie smiled, rather grimly. 'The advantages of having a female partner. You don't miss a trick.'

'Do we have ID?'

Reggie shook his head. 'Negative. No bag, no wallet, no keys, nothing. No phone either. Might have been a robbery.'

'Or made to look like one,' Jilly mused. Her eyes caught the glistening bracelet on the woman's left wrist. She pulled out a pen and gingerly lifted the tiny golden disc that dangled from it.

'If it was a robbery, they missed some of her jewelry,' Reggie observed. 'Maybe in a hurry? Or . . . maybe something else.'

She liked working with Reggie. They were usually on a similar wavelength.

'Her initials are on this: LHS.'

Reggie asked for a flashlight from the nearest uniform and bent over to look at it, shining the beam onto it.

'So they are, Red. So they are.'

'Maybe the bag's been dumped some-where close,' Jilly suggested, continuing to sweep her eyes over the body.

'They're out checking already. Anything else on her that might help ID her?'

She pulled a pair of disposable gloves out of her own pocket and donned them, then carefully checked the pockets of the woman's coat. All she found was a stub of green cardboard with a number printed on it.

'Parking ticket?' she guessed, holding it up for Reggie. He nodded and motioned over one of the officers, who peered at it and said, 'There's a lot on the next block, might be from there.'

Jilly stood up and nodded to the waiting techs, who returned with their cameras and their equipment. She reached back into her pocket and pulled out one of the small evidence bags she always carried on a call. She carefully deposited the paper into it and sealed it up, waving it at Reggie. 'We should check this out, don'tcha think?'

'All yours. I'll give you a call if anything comes up.'

The parking lot was about a block away: it was a twenty-four-hour place, so there was still an attendant on duty. Jilly showed him her badge and ID and then the ticket. He nodded that it was indeed one of their tickets, grabbed a key, and waved for her to follow him.

The car was a silver late-model Mercedes. He handed her the key and was about to leave.

'Wait, wait a minute,' she said, halting him in his tracks. 'Do you remember who brought this car in?'

The guy was dark, bushy eyebrows and mustache, deep thoughtful eyes shrouded under a broad-peaked baseball cap. He seemed to literally chew on the question for a long minute. Then he said, 'It was a lady. Nicely dressed, very polite. Smiled at me and said, 'Thank you'.'

'Do you remember what she looked like?'

'Dark hair. Nice smile.' He thought a bit and then shrugged. 'That's about all. Oh, wait, she had glasses, I think. Yeah. I remember, they were kinda smoky-tinted. I thought that was funny for nighttime.'

'What time did she come in? Don't you punch in the time?'

'Sure,' he said. 'Be right back.' He turned and strode off towards the attendant shack. Jilly hit the button on the key and heard a low beep and a click as the doors to the Lexus opened. She opened the passenger door and peeked into the vehicle. It still had that new car smell, leather with an undertone of banana oil. Another stroke of luck: the glove compartment was not locked.

Inside she found a copy of the registration and an insurance card. The name on both was Laura Hart Spilwell.

LHS, she thought. She noted the address.

The attendant came jogging back to her with a card in his hand. He showed it to her. She had entered the lot at 9.13 p.m. Jilly told him she was going to need to take the card; they'd notify his boss in the morning. The guy seemed unfazed, just nodded and looked expectantly, thick eyebrows raised under his cap.

'One last question. She didn't say anything about how long she was going to be, anything else like that?'

'Nope, that was it.' He kept his eyebrows raised in anticipation.

Jilly held up a hand in the usual 'thanks' gesture, told him she didn't need anything else from him, and that the car would be processed and should be left untouched. In a flash, he was gone. *Must be something good on his TV in the shack*, she mused.

A quick search of the vehicle didn't turn up anything else of interest. She checked the trunk and found nothing but the usual spare and jack.

She locked it up and phoned Reggie to fill him in. He said a crew of techs would be over shortly to process the car. She waited about fifteen minutes until they arrived, making some more calls in the meantime, and then headed back to the alley.

They compared notes quickly. The techs were efficiently finishing up and there would be more news tomorrow.

'Checked out the restaurant,' Reggie told her. 'Monica's. Nice little bistro. Upscale crowd. Popular, even on a Wednesday. The manager corroborated the kid's story. Kinda liked her.' He smiled.

'I'm sure your wife would like her too,' kidded Jilly.

'Actually, she kinda resembled my wife. Same kind of scary smart. Same kind of devil in her eyes.' His smile got bigger. Jilly knew he was giving her the rib.

'She put a lid on it so nobody would leave the restaurant, huh?'

'Like I said, Red, scary smart. How many people would have that presence of mind? Everybody in there is just dining and talking like nothing happened. I got all Lavonne's information so we can go back and talk to her later.'

'I'm sure you did.' Jilly smirked. Reggie shrugged innocently. Then she gave him the complete story from the parking lot.

'Laura Hart Spilwell,' he said thoughtfully. 'I know that name.'

'I ran the name and address while I was waiting for the techs,' Jilly said. 'Her husband is Dane Spilwell. *Doctor* Dane Spilwell.'

'I know that name. Big mucky-muck surgeon.'

'Plastic surgeon, to be exact. To the rich and famous.'

Reggie shook his head. 'I guess we go talk to him.' They both reflexively looked at their watches. It was very late, but bad news never waited until morning.

★ ★ ★

Even groggy from sleep and in a bathrobe, Dane Spilwell could somehow look distinguished, confident and in control. He had a full head of fashionably-styled silvery hair over a high forehead and piercing eyes. He didn't peer through the security peephole of the door of his apartment; but, of course, the doorman had notified him that they were on the way up. He asked in a clear voice who it was and then pulled the door open.

Reggie and Jilly were ready with badges and IDs on display, and he cast a quick eye over them.

'This can't be good,' he said, glancing at his expensive wristwatch. (Jilly wondered, did he sleep in it or had he reflexively put it on when he came to

12

answer the door?) 'Is there a problem?'

'Doctor Spilwell, may we come in?' asked Reggie.

'Oh, my God. Is it Laura? She's not home yet. Has something happened to her?' Jilly noted what seemed sincere alarm in those eyes. For just a fleeting moment, he lost that confident control. Then the coolness returned.

'Please, may we come in?'

Spilwell stepped aside.

It was a penthouse apartment in a very high-end section of the city, no surprise there. The living room was huge, furnished sparely and tastefully in beige and onyx, with a deep area rug over a hardwood floor.

He motioned them to a comfortable sofa and sat down in a large soft seat across a glass table from them, looking anxious and expectant.

This never got any easier. Reggie took the lead and broke the news of finding Laura's body, then offering his condolences.

Jilly thought Spilwell took the news surprisingly well. Taking a while for it to set in? Shock? A devastated man trying to remain stoic? Or was it something else? He stared down at his hands, muttered 'Oh my God,' and then after a silence began asking simple direct questions: what happened to her, where was she, did they know who did it. They answered him as directly as they could.

Dane Spilwell was high-profile, with a reputation for a patrician bearing and an icy, detached demeanor. Was this, Jilly wondered, just his personality? She had to admit, she didn't run in social circles like his, and had a certain antipathy towards this kind of high-born coolness.

Reggie's phone sounded. He excused himself and went into the corner to answer it while Jilly continued to question Spilwell, marveling at the lack of emotion in his answers. Now she had her notebook out, making notes as they talked.

'Do you know where your wife was going tonight?'

'She had her usual book group, I believe. They meet Wednesdays, rotating hosts.'

'Where was she going tonight exactly?'

'I think it would have been the home of Maura St. Ashby.' He mentioned an address in an expensive residential neighborhood to the north. Not the urban environment where Laura had been found.

'We'll need the names of the other members of that group, if you have them.'

Spilwell waved a hand absent-mindedly, looked sideways at nothing in particular. He seemed almost bored by this line of questioning.

'Of course. I think I can provide you with all of them.'

'It's awfully late. Was it unusual for her not to be home by now, or did she tend to make a late night of it?'

He glanced at his watch again. 'Sometimes they would go out for drinks or just, you know, a girls' night out kind of thing; but no, by now she would usually have been home. I would have perhaps been concerned and called her, but I had fallen asleep until just now.'

'So you were home tonight?'

'Yes. Things have been exceedingly hectic at my office and the hospital of

15

late. I made a point of coming home around eight.'

'Was Mrs. Spilwell still here or had she left already?'

'No, she had gone already.'

'Did she tend to leave a note for you or anything when she left, maybe send you a text — just to say *goodbye, see you later*?'

Spilwell sighed as if trying to make sense to a fool, or perhaps just a lower-class peon. 'No, we didn't tend to leave each other little love notes, Detective, or anything like that. We apprised one another of our schedules regularly and we both knew what the other would be doing on any given day.'

Jilly said nothing, but the expression 'piece of work' came to mind as she kept her head down and jotted a few more notes. Then she raised her head again as Reggie returned and rejoined her on the couch.

'So you went to sleep, you said. Around what time would that be?'

'Let me see. I was tired tonight. As I said, I had an exhausting week. I had a brandy, read a bit, probably fell asleep sometime around, oh, I'd say ten.'

'And you were asleep until we woke you now?'

Spilwell nodded. 'But why are we talking about me? Aren't there any avenues of inquiry you'd like to explore about what happened to Laura?'

'Absolutely, sir,' Reggie replied, working his way back into the questioning. 'Can you think of any reason she would have been in that neighborhood tonight? That's nowhere near the destination you mentioned.'

'I have no idea.'

'There are a lot of restaurants nearby. You said sometimes the group turned it into a girls' night out. Perhaps something like that?'

He thought about that. 'I know Monica's is near there somewhere. We would go there on rare occasions. She liked that it was small and intimate and had a surprisingly good wine list. Otherwise, no, I can't think of much of a reason for her to have been there.'

Reggie and Jilly exchanged a quick look. Just a coincidence that Monica's had come up again? Maybe.

Reggie took the plunge. 'Doctor, this is a difficult question, forgive me, but you must understand we have to consider every possibility. Could your wife have been . . . '

'Meeting someone else? I very much doubt it, Detective. You're suggesting her book group outings were just a convenient cover for a, a tryst of some kind?' Spilwell had reacted reflexively to the question, almost indignantly.

There was a long, tense moment of silence in the large living room.

Reggie had tacitly left Jilly the opening to be the understanding one while he took the blunt, tactless role. They knew each other well. This might come in handy later. She interjected, 'I'm sorry, we do have to ask. Perhaps it would be better if we were to come back sometime later, maybe tomorrow, and ask you further questions?'

'That might be a good idea, yes,' Spilwell agreed. They exchanged contacts and a few formal pleasantries. Then Spilwell's door was shutting behind them as they made their way back to the elevator.

Reggie brought Jilly up to speed on his call. 'They already found her bag. Jammed into a trash can a block away. No phone. There was a wallet and money and credit cards still in it.'

'Convenient, don't you think?'

Reggie nodded almost imperceptibly. 'You're thinking what I'm thinking, then?'

'Made to look like a robbery. Conveniently drop the bag nearby, where it'll be found.'

'Hope a vagrant picks through it, maybe gets caught with a card or some personal article from it?'

'Let's go see what the doorman has to say.'

In the wood-paneled elevator, Reggie's phone buzzed once again. He answered it and spoke for a moment. He nodded, said, 'Thank you, officer,' and hit the 'End Call' button.

'You're not going to believe this,' he said as the elevator smoothly stopped and the door quietly slid open onto the lobby.

'So, tell me already.'

'One of the uniforms is still out there. He just found a knife.'

'What? You mean the murder weapon?'

'Well, he can't be sure yet, but would you bet against it?'

'Where was it?'

'He was looking into storm grates, sewers, things like that. He saw a glint of light and pulled up a grate and brought it out. It's a knife. With blood. Not even three blocks away.'

'It was just lying in there, like it was just dropped?'

'He said he had to crawl down and in to retrieve it. It was like it had been thrown through the grate by someone hoping it wouldn't be seen until it got flushed into the sewer.'

'Now, that's a rare break.'

'Seems that way, Red. Let's hope.'

'I don't like the doctor one bit,' Jilly said. 'Cold as ice.'

They stepped out of the elevator onto the plush carpet of the lobby and walked toward the uniformed doorman standing at the entrance, eyeing them with curiosity.

★ ★ ★

One year later, Kerry Moran would still recall that September night vividly.

'They tell me,' Kerry was telling Mark as he held her hand across the table, 'that this place is the scene for more marriage proposals than any other restaurant in town.'

'Is that a suggestion?' Mark smiled back.

'You think we're ready for that?'

Mark laughed. 'Well, who knows? Maybe. But this is a pretty cool place. I'll definitely keep it in mind for when the time is right.' It was a small, intimate restaurant, lit by candlelight, three cozy rooms with tables for two, spaced for privacy. They were in the smallest of the rooms, just themselves and two other couples. There was a low murmur of voices, the occasional clink of a wine glass.

Mark lifted his champagne glass and tilted it toward Kerry. 'Happy anniversary, my dear.'

She picked up her own glass and mirrored his gesture, smiling. 'One year.

And they said it couldn't be done.'

'So, are you lovebirds ready to order?' asked the lean figure in black shirt and pants who had suddenly materialized alongside them.

'Need a couple more minutes, Satch,' Kerry replied to him, looking down at the menu splayed open in front of her. 'We've just been talking about true love and important things like that. A perfect setting for it, don't you think?'

Satch made a face and bent down with a conspiratorial look on his face. He spoke softly, almost in a whisper. 'To tell you the truth, there's always a lot of romance going on in here, but it's not always of the 'true' variety, if you catch my drift?'

Kerry matched his whisper as if in collusion. 'Satch, I'm shocked. You mean to tell me there are, what do you call them, trysts and assignations getting underway here?' She opened her eyes wide theatrically. Mark watched with amusement. These two had been friends for a while and shared a flair for the dramatic.

The waiter bent closer, as if explaining a menu item. 'I'm not supposed to tell you this, it's highly unprofessional,' he said, rolling his eyes to his right and tilting his head ever so slightly. 'But that other couple I'm waiting on are *definitely* an item.'

Kerry turned her head — subtly, she hoped — in the indicated direction. In the low light, she could just make out the rather distinguished-looking fellow in the stylish dark grey suit with the full head of silvery hair. His partner had her back turned to them, but Kerry could see the spectacular shade of red of her hair, the subdued green of her obviously expensive dress, and the deep green glint of a bracelet and earrings. She said to Satch, 'They look like they've been together a long time.'

'Don't kid yourself, sister. They've probably been married a long time. But not to each other.'

'Satch!' Her old friend could still shock her, even if in fun. She brought a hand to her mouth, wishing she hadn't said that quite so loud.

'No, really, wait tables long enough, you get to know this kind of stuff. Dressed to the nines — she's got on her best emeralds and that killer dress? They're shooting all these meaningful looks back and forth? They're just champing at the bit. I'm surprised they're making it through dessert. That's an affair.' He punctuated the last word with gleeful malice, straightening back up again.

'Maybe,' Mark broke in, 'if you wait tables a little longer, you'll get to know how to wait tables, stuff like that?'

'Satch, you really don't think two married people could have that kind of spark?'

He shrugged. 'Cynicism. The mark of the cosmopolitan world-weary. What can I tell you, we waiters are a jaundiced lot. Anyway, did I already mention that our chef's got a great special kale-and-ginger appetizer tonight . . . '

After Satch moved away from the table, Kerry tented her hands and rested her chin on top of them, just staring at Mark.

'So how do you know that guy again?' he asked.

'Oh, come on, Mark, I've told you about Satch. He and I went to college together.'

'Oh yeah, he's the jazz musician. Funny nickname. What would musicians do without waiting jobs?'

'He's pretty good. I bet it won't be long before he can give this up. And I guess he liked the name Satch better than his real name.'

'Uh . . . which is?'

'Mort. No kidding. Mort Blessing.'

'Mort, as in Mortimer? You're kidding!'

'Nope. I think he was named after his grandfather or someone. Probably will spend years of his life in therapy trying to forgive his parents.'

'I'd change my name, too. But not to Satch.'

'He told me where that came from. Something about bringing his horn to shows and rehearsals in a leather bag, like a satchel. The connection to Louis Armstrong, Satchmo, made it irresistible, I guess. Anyway, he was happy they stopped calling him Mort.'

'Here we are on our one-year anniversary, my love, discussing satchels and handbags. Let's start over. Lovely place. Lovely night.'

Kerry cast another glance at the twosome at the far table. The two looked so captivated in each other. She couldn't see the face of the woman in the beautiful emeralds, but the man was distinguished and dreamy-eyed, showing her his full attention as they spoke quietly. Kerry found herself fantasizing about the couple, that they enjoyed a perfectly blissful life together. She hoped Satch was wrong about them. She wanted to someday find herself in a long marriage in which she and her husband still looked at each other that way.

She had a sudden impulse and smiled mischievously at Mark, pulling out her phone. She made a motion to Satch, who once again descended upon their table.

'Hey Satch, will you do us a favor and take a couple of pictures of us?' She raised an eyebrow at Mark, who nodded in agreement.

'Of course, Madame,' Satch replied with a flourish, taking her camera phone. Kerry rose from her seat and pulled her chair around next to Mark. They struck some appropriate poses of intimate affection, then mugged self-consciously, as if to indicate they really weren't so hopelessly unhip as to be sincere about all this kind of thing. Satch took four or five quick photos. Mark dipped his head to plant a kiss on her temple just as one of the shots flashed.

It was a wonderful moment and all seemed right with the world. She and Mark were in love, everybody smiled and laughed, and even the sweet enraptured couple across the room from them looked to be in their own paradise. *If only*, she thought, *life could always be so sweet.*

2

'Hey, you're reading that story *again*?' Dan was saying, interrupting her concentration. She put down the open newspaper and looked across her desk at him. The squad room was full of noise and hustle: voices, phones, vague computer noises. It was a typical morning at the Personal Crimes Unit.

'This brought back a lot,' Jilly said.

'I remember the case too. Don't forget, I was still a patrolman.'

'How could I forget? You're the one who found the knife. Probably how you got your nice new detective badge.'

'That paper's five days old now,' Dan said, pointing at the open newspaper. 'Brings back memories of Reggie, I get it.'

Jilly shook her head. 'Maybe a little bit. But I'm not going to burden my new partner with tales of my old one. That's like telling your husband about your ex or something.' She closed the paper up,

28

folded it and dropped it on top of her IN stack.

Dan Lee, the new guy on the unit, raised his Styrofoam cup of coffee in a peace gesture. 'No, no problem, Jilly. Reggie was a righteous cop. One of the good ones.' Jilly was already warming to Dan. He was young, smart, serious. He was first generation Chinese-American, and his immigrant family was immensely proud of his success and dedication. 'I'm not expecting to replace him. I couldn't. Nobody could. For the record, I'm really happy they made me your partner.'

'Thanks for that,' said Jilly. 'I'm sorry, Dan, I need to move on.'

'At least there's some closure. That guy got convicted. Even that snake-oil sales-man of a lawyer, Towers, couldn't spin it any different. Jury didn't even deliberate all that long.'

'He'll appeal. We know Towers. He'll definitely appeal.'

'Still,' Dan mused, taking a sip of the black coffee, 'a conviction is a conviction.' He paused a beat to swallow. 'Was that the last case you and Reg worked on?'

'The last major one.'

Detective Frank Vandegraf walked by and laid a hand on Jilly's shoulder, nodding greetings to Dan. He had just returned from four days' vacation and it was his first chance to talk to her since the news had come down.

'Good news,' he said quietly. 'Reg would be very happy.'

Jilly just nodded and patted Frank's hand. He moved on to his own desk and the pile of cases and reports that had amassed in his absence.

'So what's up today?' Dan asked, draining the cup and looking around for a waste basket.

'The usual pain in the neck stuff,' muttered Jilly. 'That aggravated assault case is getting stale, maybe we need to re-canvass . . .'

The phone on her desk rang.

'Garvey,' she spoke into it briskly.

'This is Mallory, down at the desk. There's someone here to see you, Detective Garvey.' Mallory, an old-school adjutant if ever there was one, muffled the receiver with his hand and asked a question of the visitor. 'She says her name is Kerry Moran, and she wants to talk to the detective who worked the Spilwell case.'

'Really,' was all Jilly could bring herself to say.

'That would be you, correct?'

'Uh, yes. It would.'

'So, can I send her up?'

'I guess so,' Jilly sighed. She hung up the receiver, pulled the four-day old newspaper back out from the pile and opened it up once again. She couldn't help it.

The headline screamed out in large-point type:

SPILWELL GUILTY.

In smaller type beneath, but still screaming:

TO BE SENTENCED TUESDAY

She scanned several of the sentences, skipping here and there across the page. She had read this many times by now, but it still had the impact of a first read.

'An extensive trial that has rocked the city finally concluded today, almost exactly one year to the day after the shocking murder of socialite wife Laura Hart Spilwell, when a jury of seven women and five men found Dr. Dane Spilwell guilty of first-degree murder after less than six hours of deliberation . . .

'Spilwell, 58, a noted plastic surgeon and community figure, shook his head in disbelief as the jury foreman read the verdict . . .

'Spilwell's lawyer, Norland Towers, called the verdict a miscarriage of justice. He maintained his client's innocence and said there would be an appeal of the verdict . . .'

'What's going on?' asked Dan.

'I'm not quite sure,' Jilly said. She looked up to see a young woman being directed in her general direction. She figured it would be a good idea to meet her part way and rose to head her off. 'I'll be right back.'

An earnest young woman at that, Jilly

figured: intelligent hazel eyes, shoulder length brown hair styled in a no nonsense haircut, decidedly non-flashy skirt and sweater. Kerry Moran shook Jilly's hand firmly, introduced herself and asked for a few minutes of her time. Jilly saw no reason to commandeer an interview room so she steered her to an empty desk and pulled over an additional rolling chair.

'What can I do for you, Miss Moran?'

She laid her briefcase on the desk in front of her. 'You're the detective who worked on the Spilwell murder case?'

'I was one of them, yes.'

'I saw the news that he was convicted the other day.'

'Yes, he was.'

'I think that he might be innocent.'

Jilly couldn't help herself. She ran a hand down her face and took a deep breath.

'It must seem strange that I'd come to you, but . . . '

'It's more than strange,' Jilly interrupted. 'You're talking to the person who saw all the evidence. In fact I'm the one who *gathered* it. I don't know what it is you think you've got, but, believe me, he did it, Miss Moran.'

'Can I just tell you what I've got, *show* you?'

'Miss Moran, why don't you go talk to Dane Spilwell's attorney? He's the one who might be interested in whatever you think you know.'

'I tried. Norland Towers, his lawyer. I called, I went to his offices. He won't see me. I spoke to one of his associates but she basically gave me short shrift, blew me off.'

Short shrift, thought Jilly, now there's an expression you don't hear much anymore. She had a well-educated cuckoo here at very least. Murder case groupies and aficionados were a common phenomenon but this one was different from the usual array. That was probably why Mallory had let her through.

'I found that puzzling,' she continued. 'Wouldn't you think they'd want to see anything that would help in an appeal?'

'Miss Moran, not to be rude, but I'm pretty busy right now. I don't think I'm the one you should be talking to about this.' Jilly started to get up from the desk.

'I saw Dane Spilwell,' Kerry blurted out, her eyes blazing indignantly. 'I saw him the night he was supposed to have killed his wife.'

'Really. And for a year you never came forward or said anything?'

'I didn't realize it. Not until now.'

'Excuse me?'

Kerry reached into the portfolio case and pulled out a large glossy photo-print. She held it out to Jilly, who glanced down at it. In the lower left corner there were two smiling people, one of whom appeared to be Kerry herself. The man in the photo had bent his head toward her and over his shoulder could be seen another couple seated at a table. The setting seemed to be a dimly-lit restaurant. There was a man facing the camera and a woman with her back to it.

Kerry pulled out a second photo and held it up. This was a blow-up of part of the first and appeared to have been manipulated digitally to sharpen the features. The man in the background was larger, brighter, and clearer.

'I enhanced this as best I could,' Kerry said. 'Tell me that is not Dane Spilwell.'

Jilly looked at the picture and shrugged.

'This was taken at a restaurant called Light in the Tower at nine fifteen on the night of Wednesday the eighteenth of September of last year. The night that he allegedly killed his wife.'

'Miss Moran, this doesn't prove anything.'

'I was there and I saw them. I remember him, and when I saw the photos on TV and online, I knew it was him! And look. That wasn't his wife he was with, is it? I saw pictures of the wife, but that is *not* her.'

Jilly rolled her eyes and sighed. She hated when the victim was minimized in any way. ''The wife,' as you put it? Her name was Laura. And all you have is this . . . doctored photo from where, your phone?'

'It's not *doctored*. It's *enhanced*. I uploaded it from my phone, yes, to my computer and sharpened and clarified it. I'm a graphic designer. That's what I do.'

She had set her jaw and was almost glaring up at Jilly.

'I was there. I saw them.' She caught herself and paused. 'He was having an affair with a woman, she was likely also married. That's why the news stories said he couldn't provide an alibi for where he was that evening. He was protecting her.'

'Even if there were any truth to this, which I doubt, what exactly did you expect would come from telling me about it, Miss Moran?'

That gave Kerry pause. 'I . . . don't really know, I'm trying everything I can think of. I just thought, well, you're a detective. Maybe there would be something you could . . . '

Jill sat back down again, controlling the rising exasperation she felt. She silently counted to seven. She would never have made ten. 'Okay, look, I'm going to take a few more minutes and just explain something to you, and then I really need to get back to being a detective.' She stared directly at Kerry and spoke rapidly, her hands moving with the energy of her frustration.

'My partner and I were the ones who assembled all the facts. Nobody knew more about what happened that night than we did. Nobody. The night that Laura Spilwell died, nobody saw or heard from Dane Spilwell all evening. Nobody was able to confirm what time he might have left his office. He claimed he was home but even his doorman couldn't corroborate that. But there *was* video from a camera in his building garage showing him coming in late that night. We found the knife that killed Laura. Definite match to blood and stab wounds. The knife belonged to Dane Spilwell, from a kitchen set in his apartment. There was more, much more. There were means, there was motive, there was opportunity. That's how we work, Miss Moran. There's also something called experience. My partner and I have both worked lots of murder cases and there were signs, so *many* signs, that Dane Spilwell was guilty as sin of murdering his wife. On top of that, he was defended in court by Norland Towers, who is one of the most successful criminal defense attorneys in the business, and even Towers couldn't sway a jury from being overwhelmingly convinced of his guilt.'

Jilly handed the photos back to Kerry, who sat frozen, mouth partly open, looking abashed. 'Miss Moran, you said you're a designer, that's what you do? I'm a cop. That's what I do. My job is to find the bad guys and make sure they're punished, and I think I'm extremely good at it. That's what I did in this case and there is no doubt in my mind we got the right guy.'

She stood up and composed herself.

'Thank you for coming in. I'm afraid I can't be of any help and my advice is to forget about this, because you're on a misguided mission. Leave this to the professionals. Dane Spilwell is guilty.'

She nodded and turned to walk away, leaving Kerry sitting at the desk holding the prints.

Dan looked up from his desk as Jilly approached. 'So what was that all about?'

'Waste of time,' muttered Jilly. 'Total waste of time. So what do you think about doubling back on some of those leads on the assault?'

3

The Personal Crimes Unit was always, it seemed, ablaze with activity. The city generously dropped new serious crime into their laps on a regular basis. Years earlier, the unit had been called Special Crimes and before that had gone by the prosaic but accurate Robbery-Homicide. At some point the Department had decided Personal Crimes bore more gravitas. The unit still dealt with basically the same types of crime, almost entirely felonies: homicides, severe assaults, robberies. Simultaneously, the unit that handled burglaries and similar non-violent crimes had gained the moniker Property Crimes and was currently housed in a similar squad room one flight up from Personal Crimes. Jilly, in her years in the unit, had never noticed any great difference in anything except the name.

Jilly arrived at her desk early and

dropped the newspaper on her desk. The headline read SPILWELL SENTENCED TO LIFE. She looked at the two telephone message slips greeting her. Both were from Kerry Moran.

Now what? She shook her head and pressed her temples. Wasn't it too early to be getting a headache?

She hadn't even sat down before her desk phone was buzzing.

'Garvey.'

'Detective Garvey, it's Kerry Moran.'

Jilly took a deep breath. 'Yes, Miss Moran, what's up?'

'I've had threats made against me is what!'

'Excuse me?'

'I said I've been threatened, Detective, and it has to do with my involvement in the Dane Spilwell case!'

Another deep breath. 'You are *not* 'involved' in the case, Miss Moran. Now tell me just how you've been threatened?'

'I got the call late last night.' Kerry sounded distraught and a bit addled. 'A man telling me to lay off.'

'Lay off?'

41

'Lay off trying to convince people that Dane Spilwell is innocent!'

'I've told you, you shouldn't be doing that anyway! Who was the person who called you?'

'I don't know, I have no idea! He didn't identify himself, just told me I should stop, and then he hung up.'

'That hardly sounds like a threatening call.'

'At two in the morning?'

'Kerry, you need to drop this whole thing. What's the matter with you?'

'Detective, I'm sure he's innocent. I need to find someone who will believe me.'

A third deep sigh was the last that Jilly was going to allow herself. She had to end this conversation, and this problem, before she either hyperventilated or exploded.

'All right, look, where are you right now? Are you far from me?'

'No, I'm about eight or nine blocks away in a coffee house. The JavaBean, on Henley?'

'Okay, I want you to wait for me, I'm

going to come over and we are going to have a *short* talk, okay?'

'Really? Sure! I'll wait for you!'

Jilly dropped the phone down, shaking her head. Dan had just arrived, in time to catch the tail end of the conversation.

'What was that all about?'

'It's that stupid little Moran girl again. I'm going to go try to explain reality to her in person.'

'She's still on the Spilwell kick?'

'And she's making a nuisance of herself in the process. I hate it when people want to go all Nancy Drew on us.'

'I'm surprised you're taking the time to go see her.'

'I need to lay this out in the strongest possible terms. Or else one of these days we're going to be bringing her in.'

'Have fun,' smiled Dan. 'I'll catch us up on some of our reports in the meantime.'

'Appreciate that,' muttered Jilly as she grabbed her bag and jacket and prepared to head back out of the squad room.

★ ★ ★

Jilly had grabbed a double Americano and now sat down across from Kerry, who looked as if she hadn't slept much recently. She was pale, shaking, looking around furtively.

'Thank you for coming,' she said.

'I'm not going to be here long. I'm just going to explain a few things to you and hope to drive some sense into your head. What have you been doing since you came to the station anyway?'

'Like I said, I've been trying to find someone who will listen to me!'

'Kerry, I've told you there is no question he's guilty! None at all! Why are you so sure he's innocent, getting yourself all worked up over this nonsense?'

Kerry's eyes got big and watery all of a sudden as she stared at Jilly, reminding her of more than one soap opera actress. 'If you had been there, you would have understood. He was totally taken with her, the woman with the emeralds and the red hair — kind of like yours, in fact, except it just sparkled and glowed, like fire! It was spectacular!'

Thanks a lot, thought Jilly, catching

herself unconsciously raising a hand to her own short ruddy hair.

'The way he was looking at her — he wasn't leaving her that evening! And it was definitely the same man in the photos I saw from the trial!'

This was making no sense to Jilly whatsoever.

'I guess . . . ' Kerry looked down, shook her head and made a strange smile. 'I guess I need to still believe in real love.'

'Let me get this straight. You think you saw Dane Spilwell having dinner with another woman, not his wife. You're saying he was cheating on his wife Laura that evening.'

'Yes, that's what I'm saying.'

'And you want to believe that he was cheating because . . . you desperately want to believe in true love?'

'Exactly!' Kerry said excitedly. She stared earnestly. 'People cheat, yes. People make mistakes. They find themselves with the wrong people. I'm not saying that any of that is right, hurting others, betraying their trust, but isn't it possible to decide that the person you truly love is somebody else, not the person you're with?'

'Oh my God, Kerry, How old are you anyway? Sixteen?'

'I'm twenty-four,' she replied defensively. 'What difference does that make?'

'You do realize, don't you, how totally ridiculous your argument sounds? Especially to a cop like me?'

Kerry shrugged.

Jilly tried to find another line of communication. She reached over and touched Kerry's hand and stared into her eyes. 'Why is this so important to you? Do you know Dane Spilwell?'

'No.'

'Did you know his wife? Anybody in his family?'

'Oh, no.'

'Then what?'

Kerry waited a minute, as if trying to gather her thoughts, dropping her gaze down at her hands. 'Last year, when I was at that restaurant and saw that couple, I had a boyfriend and we were in love. I had a great job. The world was just wonderful.' She looked up at Jilly. 'Right now? I've got nobody, no job, nothing. I really need to believe that what I saw in that room last year was real. That that man loved that woman so much that he wouldn't have left her for anything that night. That he would ultimately sacrifice himself for her. He never gave anybody an alibi for his time that night, did he?'

Jilly shook her head. 'No.'

'That's because he didn't want to jeopardize the woman he loved. I bet she's married too. He's protecting her.'

Jilly wanted to say, Dane Spilwell is a slimebag, a selfish, arrogant lowlife covered in the trappings of the high life. He's no knight in shining armor. But she decided it wasn't worth it.

'Kerry, who have you talked to about this?'

'Besides Norland Towers? Or rather his associate, Ms. Grymes? Well . . . nobody at the Blade-Courier would talk to me. I left email messages with three different reporters there. His brother would have no part of it . . . '

'Wait a minute. His brother?'

'Yeah. Ryan Hart.'

'How did you find him?'

'Actually, he found me. He called me and asked me to meet him in the park. He said that this was dragging up terrible things for the family, that he appreciated my efforts but they would actually cause more harm than good. The whole meeting lasted maybe five or ten minutes. He said I shouldn't try to reach him or any of the family, not ever. He said I didn't realize the harm I was causing. He just kept saying to trust him, I didn't understand. He was right, I didn't understand. How could it be harmful if it cleared his brother?'

'Did he tell you how to reach him?'

'Oh, no, he said he never wanted to hear from me ever again.'

Now Jilly was interested. 'Who else did you talk with?'

'Well, I tried to reach Satch, the waiter from the restaurant, but he quit. We used to be good friends but we hadn't talked in a while now.' She took a deep breath. 'And then I tried Mark.'

'Mark?'

'Mark Zanello. He . . . was with me

that night. He won't answer my calls.' Another pause. It seemed as if Kerry was going to cry. 'Can't blame him for that.' She sniffed a little and changed the subject. 'And then there was Clea Solana.'

'Clea Solana? You actually tried to talk to *her*? In heaven's name, why?'

'You know her then?'

'Not personally, no. But Kerry . . . ' Jilly shook her head in utter frustration at this dingbat sitting in front of her. 'Kerry, you can't just go around stalking people like that, just because they're famous! You're lucky you haven't been arrested or slapped with a restraining order!'

Clea Solana was the wife of a world famous film director, a filmmaker herself as well as a patroness of the arts. They were both highly prominent in the society of many major cities throughout the world. She and her husband maintained a residence in this very city, among many other international locales.

'Not stalking, I just wanted to talk to her. You know her history with Dane Spilwell, don't you?'

'Yes, of course I do.'

It was a bizarre, sad story told in gossipy whispers. Clea Solana had pursued cosmetic surgery for years in search of beautification. Dane Spilwell had been her most recent plastic surgeon and something had gone tragically wrong. At the end Clea, rather than being transformed into Beauty personified, had been turned into something more closely resembling a Beast. Clea had continued to carry on her high profile international business, in the spotlight and the society columns. Everybody involved acted as if there were nothing whatsoever unusual about her appearance. A new retelling of the Emperor's New Clothes. The super-rich could lead very different lives indeed, even bend the very reality around them, it would seem.

'Kerry, are you insane? *Why* would you try to talk to her? Do you have any idea . . . '

'She just seemed a likely suspect, that's all. He destroyed her life, in a way.'

'So you were going to, what, confront her? Accuse her? You stupid girl! Do you realize what could have happened?'

'I said I was doing a feature on her for a magazine. I used the name of my former employer, the magazine I worked for. I was posing a fluff interview, hoping to maybe catch some clue if I could catch her with her guard down. But I couldn't get anywhere near her. I was turned down cold at the lowest levels.'

'You honestly thought Clea Solana could have killed Laura Spilwell?'

'She was in town that week, I checked. She was here for an art opening. As you would say, she had motive, she hated the Spilwells, wouldn't you? She had opportunity. I figured it was as good a shot as I had.'

Kerry pulled a familiar photo out of her bag and dropped it on the table. She stabbed it with a finger.

'This man I saw, he was Dane Spilwell. And he did not kill his wife.'

'Kerry, one question that I keep wondering about? Why did you wait until now to bring all this up? Your photo is a year old. The case was in the news. You had to know about this then. And you didn't come forward, you did nothing.'

'I never made the connection until now! This has been a, well, a pretty stressful year for me. I was distracted. My mind was elsewhere. Then I was going through old photos on my phone, finally getting rid of them. It was a, a kind of anniversary this week. Good memories turned bad. Not worth going into right now. I saw that picture and it brought up a whole chain of memories, you know how something can do that? I had the TV on and the news was showing Dane Spilwell's picture. It was just a coincidence. And all of a sudden it made sense.' She stabbed the photo once again with her finger. 'It was him. I'm positive.'

Jilly took the photo and looked at it. 'You need to promise me you will stop trying to do police work *now*.'

'Are you going to take me seriously and look into this?'

'No, but I will look into this alleged threat you received last night.'

'*Alleged!*' Kerry almost yelled.

'I'm not saying I don't believe someone called you last night. I'm just saying there's no grounds for characterizing it legally as a threat. So tell me exactly what this person said to you.'

'Well, he woke me up. As I said, it was like around two in the morning. He asked if he was speaking to Kerry and I said yes. Then he said, 'You're going to make a lot of trouble for yourself, you need to lay off this thing you've taken on for yourself.' I asked him what thing he was talking about and he said, 'You know what I'm talking about. Give up on it right now.' I asked who he was but he just hung up. That was it.'

'What did his voice sound like?'

'Low, gruff, he was kind of whispering hoarsely. I didn't recognize it, it was nobody I had ever spoken with. Or maybe he was disguising it.'

'This was on a land line?'

'No, I don't have one, only my mobile.' A common situation: more people, especially younger ones, were dropping their land lines in favor of cells as rates increased.

'And you've been giving out your number in your travels, I assume?'

'Yeah. Maybe not such a great idea, but . . . '

'All right, does your phone record incoming calls?'

'Yes, of course,' Kerry said, punching up the record and showing the screen to Jilly.

'I'd like you to take a screen shot of that and message it to me, okay?' She gave Kerry her number and had her send it right then. 'And don't delete those records. I'll see if I can run anything down from this number. I may need your official okay that I could do all this, just in case. Oh by the way . . . could I see your record of the call you received from the brother?'

'Sure,' said Kerry, now punching that up and turning the screen to Jilly.

'Send me that one too, would you?' Jilly said, writing as she spoke. 'And keep it.'

'Sure.'

'I can't promise anything, but I will look into it for you.'

'This time, do you want to keep this?' Kerry asked, handing her the photo. 'I've got plenty of copies.'

'Yeah, why not,' Jilly said, not really quite sure why except that it might pacify Kerry a little bit. She stood up, signaling the meeting was over.

'Now listen to me. I'm serious. You need to tell me you are *not* going to play detective anymore with this stuff. You're going to drop it completely and let me look into this. I don't think you are in any danger, but I *do* think you could still get yourself in a world of trouble. So do I have your word?'

Kerry, looking abashed, nodded and said, 'Okay. I promise. I won't do anything more about this until I hear from you.'

'Not ever!' Jilly replied sternly. 'I want to hear it from you!'

'Agreed.'

'I have to run, Kerry. I'll call you about anything that comes up from these phone calls.' She grabbed her bag and tossed her empty cup into the trash as she headed for the door.

On the street the ringtone of her phone erupted in her pocket, a snippet of music by Stravinsky she had just added. It was Dan.

'Hey, partner, I'm on my way back.'

'Actually, I need you to meet me,' Dan said. 'We got a body.' He gave her an address.

'On my way,' she breathed, realizing just how exhausting that short conversation with that crazy girl had been.

★　★　★

'Kinda looks like nobody expected us to find him for a long time,' the female officer was saying. 'After he was shot, someone stuck him back in that building.'

They stood on the stoop of a broken down brick edifice that had obviously been abandoned for some time. Its windows were boarded up. The wooden front door, paint peeling and hinges rusting, was jammed partially open.

The medical examiner's van was just pulling up. The officer led Dan into the building. They were careful not to touch the door and to watch where they walked, picking their way over the dusty debris on the floor. It had been a residential building some years ago, and they entered into a hallway leading to a large room, likely designed to be a parlor.

There was some light coming through the cracks in the window boards but it did not penetrate to the next room back, possibly once a bedroom. A second officer stood there, directing a flashlight down onto the ground, dust particles flitting chaotically in the beam.

They worked their way through the dark to look down at what was captured in the shaft of light. A man, not a very old one, lay on his back, eyes wide open in a death stare at the ceiling. Blood had pooled beneath his head. The odor was already unpleasant.

The MEs were slamming the doors to the van and heading up the stoop with their equipment. Dan yelled out for them to show caution; the SID techs hadn't yet arrived.

'Maybe a gang killing,' the female officer said. 'Maybe an initiation. But it's kind of odd. Two bullets in the head, from first look.'

'Doesn't look like a gangbanger,' Dan reflected, crouching down to get a better look at the body in the flashlight's beam. 'Not with those clothes. This looks more like an urban hipster.'

The officer, whose nametag read KOVETSKY, shrugged. 'Trying to buy drugs, maybe?'

'Right neighborhood for it,' said Dan, not looking up. He had already snapped on a pair of latex gloves and was very gingerly lifting the dead man's jacket, looking for identification or anything else that might suggest who he was.

'Just wrong place, wrong time maybe,' she offered.

'Look at his fingernails,' Dan muttered, lifting a hand slightly. 'Clipped carefully. The hands look soft, and they're reasonably clean.' Not a gang member. Likely not a junkie. A young professional looking for pot or coke or . . . ?

'Who found him?' Dan asked.

'Homeless couple snuck in here early this morning. They forced the door. Well, they won't admit that, but it sure looks like they did.'

'And they called it in?'

'Yeah, how about that,' said Officer Kovetsky. 'They got a cell phone!'

'Where are they?'

'Those two sitting on the stoop a couple doors down. I bought them a couple cups of coffee and asked them to hang around.'

'Nice of you,' Dan nodded.

'I know 'em, they're regulars in this neighborhood. I didn't want them to bolt. I told them they were in no trouble. I'd say they trust me. I honestly can't see them having anything to do with this.'

'Good thinking. Maybe they know or saw something, it's worth a try.'

The medical examiners filled the room and some lights came on as they set up their portable illumination. The room somehow looked even more drab and dreary in the sun-bright arc lighting. There was more noise outside as more vehicles arrived and more feet came up the steps. Scientific Investigation Division techs were arriving, along with somebody else, Dan was happy to note.

'Hey partner,' came Jilly's voice as she

stepped into the room. 'What've we got here?'

'Come check it out, Jilly.'

'Officer Kovetsky, how are you doing?' Kovetsky nodded back at her. Dan began filling Jilly in on what he had already learned as he continued to search the body. He found something jammed deep into the man's pants pocket and delicately tried to maneuver it out. There were folded up envelopes.

'Doesn't seem to be a wallet or ID,' Dan said. 'This is all that was in his pocket.' He unfolded them and held them up in the light.

'This one's just junk mail . . . this one's an electric bill. Maybe he had grabbed his mail leaving his home.' Dan read the name off the front of the bill. 'Mark . . . Zanello, looks like? 4356 West Brophy, Apartment 314. He's pretty far away from home.'

'Wait a minute,' Jilly said abruptly. 'His name is Mark Zanello?'

'I'd guess it's his, yeah. In any case that's the name on the . . . '

Jilly tried to say them under her breath,

but the cuss words came out clearly audible. Dan looked up with a start.

'That's unlike you,' he said dryly.

'Can I see that?'

By now she was standing directly behind him. Dan passed it up to her. The ranking ME cleared his throat to indicate they were waiting to get to the body. Dan stood up and they both stepped back.

'I can't believe this,' Jilly was saying, staring at the envelope. 'This could be that crazy girl's boyfriend.'

'Come again?'

'She said she's been trying to reach him for several days and he never answered or returned her calls,' Jilly said, slightly dazed, struggling to make sense of this.

'This would certainly be a good excuse,' Dan replied.

'How long would you say he's been here?' Jilly asked the coroner's man.

'I'll be able to give you a better answer in a little while,' he grunted, 'but judging from what I'm seeing here, maybe four or five days.'

'This is an insane coincidence,' she said. She took out her phone and snapped several photos of the body, especially the face, trying to get an angle that avoided the worst of the gaping head wounds. 'And that's what it has to be.'

'Maybe we should give them some room to work,' said Dan. Jilly nodded. They moved back to the parlor, now arc-lit. The entire ground floor looked about the same: broken down, covered in dust and debris. Nothing seemed to have disturbed the pristine disorderliness except for what looked like drag marks on the floor. It seemed evident that someone had dragged the body through the hall and parlor, dumped it in the bedroom and left.

'How do you get upstairs?' Jilly asked, looking up at the ceiling.

'There's a separate stairway, has its own door outside. If somebody came in here they might not have had occasion to go up there. We can look and see if that door looks forced as well.'

Jilly paced around for another minute or two. 'This looks like a dead end in here. Might as well leave it for the techs to check out.' She headed for the front again. Dan was a step ahead of her.

Kovetsky walked them to the couple sitting on a stoop a few doors away. The man was tall, weathered, and had a thick dark beard. His female companion was equally weathered and scowling, puffing away at the remains of a cigarette. Empty coffee cups lay alongside them.

'Thanks for waiting for us, Nate. These detectives got a few questions for you, okay?' The man nodded.

'I'm Detective Garvey, this is Detective Lee. So you found the body in the building?'

'Yeah,' Nate answered in a deep raspy voice. 'We were looking for someplace to crash, it's gettin' cold lately. Usually these buildings along here, they're nailed up shut pretty tight. This one had been pried open so we looked inside.'

'And you found the body?'

'It was back in that room, where you guys saw. It was dark and we kinda stumbled over it. Soon's Nadine saw it, she started freakin' out and we got outa there.'

'You weren't too happy to find it

neither,' Nadine interjected sourly, then returned to her cigarette butt.

'How did you contact the police?' Dan asked.

Nate pulled an old flip phone out of his pocket. 'Had this for a while. I can put minutes on it when I got a couple bucks. Good for an emergency.' He showed a gap-toothed grin.

'Do you come across something like this much?'

'No, man, this was the very first time we ever found someone been murdered! Looks like he might been, what, shot?'

'Yes,' Jilly replied. 'You know any of the gangs around here?'

'Sorta. Roland 29's are the big one.' The detectives were familiar with them, homing in around 29th Street not too far from there. The name had evolved as a corruption of 'Rolling' 29s.

'So, you found the door had been pried open already when you got to it this morning?'

'Yeah, exactly. Had to give it a good shove, but . . . '

'Any other signs of anybody having

gone through the building that you could tell?'

'Hard to tell, it was all messed up in there to begin with.'

'Did you go into any of the other rooms?'

'No, when we got back there, we just turned and got out.'

'Did you go in any other places, upstairs, in any of the other buildings?'

'Nope, that was the only one that was open.'

The conversation did not get any more fruitful and after a few more questions, they thanked the couple and told them they could leave. Jilly handed Nate one of her cards.

'If you happen to think of anything else you think might be of help, just give me a call, okay? I appreciate it.'

Nate cleared his throat.

'Yeah, what?' asked Dan.

'Any chance you might be able to help us out a little?'

Dan and Jilly looked at each other. Dan pulled out his wallet and handed a bill to Nate.

'If you come up with anything else, let us know, okay?' he said as the bill changed hands.

★ ★ ★

'What do you think, partner?' Jilly asked as they walked away.

'Pretty clear those two had nothing to do with this. Maybe a gang shooting, I don't know. Doesn't feel quite right, but . . . '

'Agreed,' said Jilly. 'Can't rule out wrong place, wrong time just yet, but it's weird. I'm thinking the body was dumped from somewhere else.'

She still had the photo in her bag that Kerry had handed her earlier. She pulled it out and looked at the young man leaning over in the corner of the blowup. It was hard to be certain, but it could be the same person they had just seen on the floor of the building. She took her phone out of her pocket with a deep sigh. 'I guess we have to go talk to Kerry again.'

'I'll meet you there,' Dan said. 'No way I'm leaving my car in this neighborhood.'

Kerry answered her phone immediately.

'Kerry, it's Detective Garvey. I really need to talk to you again right away. Have you got some time right now?'

'Detective, time is pretty much all I have right now. I just got home, come on over.' She gave Jilly an address.

Jilly broke the connection and looked at Dan. 'I have a feeling this is not going to be a pleasant conversation.'

It was not a pleasant conversation. They had gone to Kerry's apartment and sat down around a kitchen table, and Jilly had shown her the photo on her phone, the one that only showed his face, his eyes having been closed. She had told Kerry how they had found him. Kerry had gone into hysterics.

It was now a good five minutes later and she was still sobbing.

'I got him killed, didn't I?' she wailed.

Jilly had put her hand on Kerry's shoulder. She said softly, 'We don't know that. This is definitely your boyfriend, Kerry? This is Mark Zanello that you told me about earlier?'

Kerry nodded her head up and down. 'He . . . he *was* my boyfriend. Not anymore.'

'I don't think this had anything to do with you. I think it's just a coincidence that we talked about him today. We're going to look into every possibility on this.'

Another minute passed and she seemed to be calming down. Dan pushed the Kleenex box a little closer to her. Finally it seemed the right moment to proceed.

'When was the last time you saw Mark?'

'A few weeks ago. Maybe a couple of months.'

'So you two haven't been together in a while?'

Kerry shook her head. 'No. No, we . . . we broke up about six months ago.'

'Have you talked in the meanwhile? Maybe on the phone, email, anything like that?'

'No. The last time we spoke was when he came by to pick up some things he had left here.'

'We're trying to make sense of where

we found him, what might have happened to him. Can you think of any reason he would have been in that neighborhood?'

'I don't know. He didn't live near there. His apartment was in a kind of sketchy area, that was becoming what you might call gentrified — but nowhere near *that* bad.'

'Did he have any friends, perhaps, who lived there?'

Kerry shook her head, looking down. 'No, nobody I know of.'

'Kerry, did Mark use any kind of drugs?'

'No, never. He drank, sometimes a bit too much, that was about it.'

'So there's no chance he was coming to see a supplier, maybe a friend or acquaintance, could that be why he was in that neighborhood?'

'Oh my God no. I can't even imagine that.'

Jilly looked at Dan, hoping he'd feel comfortable enough to jump in here. This was now their case, both of them.

'Did Mark have a car?' Dan asked.

'Sure. A Toyota, maybe five years old.'

'What does it look like?'

'It's dark green. I think it's a Matrix.'

'He was found pretty far away from where you said he lived. Would he have walked over there, possibly he was passing through the neighborhood to get somewhere else?'

'Mark wasn't much of a walker,' Kerry said. 'If he was there, he probably drove.'

'So his car might be parked nearby. We'll check into that. Might be of some help. He didn't have a wallet or identification or almost anything else on his person. No wristwatch, no jewelry, no pocket change, no keys. Would that have been normal for him, to go out without anything?'

'I can't imagine. Mark was pretty fastidious. Go out without his wallet? No.' She paused to think for a moment. 'He had an old watch, didn't like jewelry. He carried his keys in a little leather case.'

'He had an electric bill in his pocket. Would he perhaps have been on his way to pay that?'

'No, he usually paid his bills online. He had the bill in his pocket?'

'Yes, does that strike you as unusual?'

'It's just . . . strange, that's all. Maybe he got it out of his mailbox on the way out of his place?'

Jilly jumped back in again. 'Tell me about your recent relationship with Mark, would you?'

Dan took the opportunity to rise and excuse himself, saying he was going to phone in the information about Mark's car and have the uniforms check the neighborhood, see what they found. He may have been thinking Kerry would be more forthright about this if he were absent. Jilly turned back to Kerry, waiting.

'Like I said, we hadn't been together in months.'

'I'm sorry, but it might be important . . . why did you break up?'

A deep sigh from Kerry, still looking down at her hands on the table. 'Cheating.'

'He cheated on you?'

'No.' Another long pause, and she looked up at Jilly. 'I cheated on him. And he found out.'

Jilly let that play out in silence. She waited.

'I was having an affair with my boss at the magazine.'

'Uh-huh?'

'It . . . it started maybe nine months ago. It just sort of happened. Things got out of hand. I didn't plan for it to go like that. It got more and more serious, I didn't know what I wanted to do. Then Mark found out.' She made a wry, mirthless smile. 'I guess that solved the problem.'

'Were you and Mark living together at the time?'

'No, we had our separate apartments, the same ones we still have. *Had*, I guess. But I spent most of my time at his place, just came back here now and then. We had been talking about getting a place together. That was a huge step for him.' She brushed a tear away from the corner of her eye.

'We had been talking about getting *married*, for God's sake.'

'What was the breakup like? Was it . . . emotional?'

'Surprisingly, no. Not an awful lot.

Mark's not an overly demonstrative sort, it's not like he was screaming and throwing things. He keeps things in. It was more like he was hurt, really, really hurt.' The tears began once again. Jilly waited while Kerry wiped her eyes and blew her nose.

'How about you? Were you the demonstrative sort?'

'I was kind of in the wrong place to be yelling or screaming. I was the bad guy. I mostly felt guilty.' Kerry seemed then to understand the point of the question. 'Are you asking if I might have attacked Mark or something like that?'

'Just trying to get a grasp of what was happening, that's all.'

'No, no! Nothing like that! Neither of us was a violent sort! Mark never hit me or anything like that, and I certainly never did anything to him either!'

'Okay. And what about your boss, after all this came out?'

Kerry smirked. 'Almost right after that, he broke it off with me. Turns out he's 'happily married'. Things got really uncomfortable. About a week later, he fired me.'

And thus, thought Jilly, arose her desperate search to confirm real love could actually exist?

'Does Mark have any relatives in the area?'

'No, his family, what's left of it, is back East, in New York — mostly Brooklyn.'

'Where did he work?'

'For Burnt Toast. It's a small advertising and promotional firm. That was how we met. I was doing freelance work for them.' She told Jilly the address of their offices.

'How about friends, anybody he was close to?'

'About the only people I ever knew him to hang out with were Gary and Louie. He knew Louie from New York, they went back a number of years. Mark used to date Gary's sister and the two guys got to be good friends. Aside from that, well, Mark wasn't all that social. He liked to stay in, reading or playing computer games. Or watching movies. He has a huge collection of DVDs.' She caught herself. 'I . . . I guess I mean he *had*.'

'That's a perfectly normal reaction,

Kerry. Don't worry about it. Do you know how we can get in contact with Gary and Louie? Do you know their last names?'

'Yeah, Gary . . . Krasnow, I'm pretty sure is his last name. Louie, his real name is Luigi, his last name is . . . Ghirardelli. Like the chocolate. It was a joke among us.'

Dan returned to the table, tucking his phone in his pocket. 'The registration is being run for a plate, and Kovetsky's looking up and down the street for a green Matrix,' he told Jilly.

'Kerry, is there any chance that Mark tried to confront your old boss?' Jilly asked. 'You said he was very upset over the whole thing.'

'I can't see that happening. Mark wasn't like that.'

'How about your boss? Would he be capable of hurting Mark if he felt threatened?'

'I wouldn't think so, but, then, I guess I don't really know him like I thought I did, do I?'

'Could you give us his name and the

address of the magazine?'

'His name is Kevin Warfield and the magazine's *On The Spot*.' She rattled off an address including a suite number. Dan jotted it down. Kerry made an intense sneer, her eyes burning. 'You don't need to tell him hello for me or anything.'

Jilly nodded, fully comprehending.

They asked a few more questions and then wrapped up the conversation, thanking her for her help.

As they rose to leave, Kerry asked, 'So how can you be so sure that I didn't get Mark killed, asking all those questions about Dane Spilwell?'

'It just doesn't make any sense, Kerry. Don't think that way, okay? But we'll examine every possible angle. We will find out who did this to Mark.'

She felt strange making such a promise, but she had felt like she needed to do so. 'In the meantime, I have to stress again, stay away from that whole thing, stay *far* away, understood?'

Kerry nodded vigorously.

'Am I in danger, Detective?'

'I'm thinking not. Someone is trying to

discourage you from pursuing this, but there have been no express threats to you. Again, I'm inclined to believe that what happened to Mark is not related. But I do suggest you keep a low profile and stay away from this whole subject, and I'll be checking in with you regularly, and you'll be all right. Do you understand?'

Kerry nodded again.

'I'm going to be looking into those people who contacted you. Now you're sure the person who met you in the park identified himself as Laura Spilwell's brother? He said Ryan Hart?'

'That's exactly right. I remember distinctly.'

'And you said he phoned you to meet you.'

'Right.'

'When was this that he called and had you meet him?'

'Three days ago. Sunday.'

'Okay, thanks. Kerry, you'll be all right if you *do nothing* about this whole thing, don't talk to anyone, don't try to contact anyone or look into anything. I mean it!'

'I said I won't. I promise!'

'I'll see you back at the station,' Jilly said to Dan as they walked back to their cars. 'We've got a lot to talk about, to figure out how we're going to attack this one.'

Dan nodded. 'Do you really think the murder has nothing to do with this whole Dane Spilwell thing she's opened up?'

'I really doubt there's any connection, Dan. But there is one thing she told me earlier that troubles me a little.'

'The brother?'

'Yeah. Exactly. Laura Spilwell did not *have* a brother. She was an only child. And her parents are gone. In fact, there are only a couple of cousins remaining in her family.'

'Someone is going to some trouble to get Kerry to stop showing that photo around and asking questions.'

'It would seem. I still can't see a viable connection to the Mark Zanello killing. But there's something else going on there.'

'If there *is* a connection — if someone was willing to kill him to hush up whatever it is that Kerry's stumbled into — could that mean that Spilwell might really be innocent?'

'I'm not willing to buy that yet. It flies against all my instincts and experience. But . . . '

'But?' repeated Dan.

'I've just been thinking,' Jilly said, 'about something Reggie once said.'

'Which was?'

'Well, it wasn't the first time we had run across a faked robbery to cover a murder. Reggie said something like, 'It's a chess game'.'

'A chess game?' Dan repeated.

'Yeah. It's like, we see the telltale signs that the robbery is bogus, it's a red herring. We know, we can feel it sometimes. But then he'd talk about the next level of the game. When the killer wants to make it *look like* it's a setup for a fake robbery to attract attention to a third party. A double red herring.'

'Wow,' said Dan. 'I think I'm following.'

'They figure, the cops are smart enough to see through the fake and will follow through the supposed cover up, but they *aren't* smart enough to see through the higher deception. A setup of a setup. Like out of a spy novel. I can think of one time I saw something like that.'

'Really?'

'It was really heavy-handed. There was this girl named Rose. She was maybe in her early twenties, a gang member. She had it in for this other girl, a rival for the attentions of some guy she liked. So she shot her, right on a deserted street corner, just left her there. Then she left a trail to make it look like a robbery, a clumsy stupid one. She took the other girl's wallet, phone, everything, and left it all in a gutter about a half block away, after taking all the money out of the wallet. But she decided to use the opportunity to settle a second score, with an old boyfriend who had done her wrong. She had gotten hold of something personal of his — I forget what it was now — but she left it in the gutter along with the other stuff. Like he had dropped it while trying to set up the scene.'

Dan actually laughed. 'Now that takes,

I don't know, moxie?'

'Moxie?' Jilly echoed.

'You know, Guts. Daring. Audacity.'

'Yeah, well . . . it was a clumsy effort to create the impression of a clumsy effort. Didn't work for more than a few minutes. We were on it like that.' She snapped her fingers. 'The thing is, these people want to think we're not that bright, but they also think that they *are* all that smart. They're usually not.'

'So are you thinking about this in relation to the Spilwell case? Did Reggie ever think there was that extra level going on in that one?'

'No, we both had him good for that one from the start.' Jilly sighed in thought. 'At least I think we both did.'

'So the point here is . . . ?'

'I don't know. Maybe there is no point. It just came to mind, is all.'

Dan pulled his car key out of his pocket. 'Lots to think about here, isn't there? I'll see you back at the station.'

★　★　★

Dan sighed as he replaced the phone in the set on his desk. He had obtained the license plate number for Mark Zanello's aging green Toyota Matrix and called it over to Officer Kovetsky. 'She's coming up empty. Doesn't seem that the car is in that neighborhood. In fact, no Matrix of any kind.'

'Carjacking maybe?' Jilly replied from her own desk, perusing her computer screen. She had acquired Zanello's phone number and was initiating requests for records of his phone. 'Somebody grabbed his car, he put up a fight, they shot him and dumped the body?'

'Carjacking an old Matrix?' Dan asked. 'Kind of a stretch.'

Jilly shrugged. 'Most cars are boosted for parts these days, and we both know Toyotas are high on the theft lists. They're very popular cars.'

'I guess we can't rule it out,' Dan agreed. 'Just doesn't feel right.'

'My lord, what does feel right about this one?' Jilly muttered. She keyed in a SEND and looked up from her monitor. 'So let's figure out our next move.'

'I agree with you, the boss seems like a possibility. Mark's a betrayed lover, he goes to confront this Warfield guy, and things escalate.'

'Yeah. The two friends might be able to shed some light into Mark's comings and goings, maybe his state of mind. Maybe we should talk to at least one of them first, if we can — then go talk to Warfield.'

Dan nodded.

Jilly heaved a deep sigh as she picked up her phone again. 'And I'm afraid we're going to have to look into all the people that Kerry tried to contact this week, just to tie up the loose ends.'

'The lawyer, Towers.'

'Yeah. And she said she tried to talk to a couple reporters but got no further than leaving an email without any details. Probably not much there. And then there's someone who probably won't talk to me any more than they would to her.'

'What kind of reporters?'

'From the Blade. She never heard back from them.'

'I'm surprised she didn't go tabloid,'

said Dan. 'Lots of people in print and online would have run with anything if it sounded sensational.'

'Maybe if she had had more time, she might have. She was trying to find 'respectable' avenues. I'm sure she was going to keep going down the line, but then she got scared and sidelined.'

'When the threats started.'

'Or whatever they were.'

'Clearly somebody wasn't happy with what she was doing.'

'Yeah, and whether or not it's connected, I have to look into those as well.'

'We,' corrected Dan. 'We have to look into them, do I have to remind you?'

Jilly laughed. 'I stand corrected. Thanks for that. Are you sure you want to get involved in this one as well?'

'Comes with the territory.'

Jilly finished dialing and apparently someone on the other end picked up quickly. She spoke into the receiver quietly, officiously. There was a short exchange, during which she nodded several times, and then she hung up, giving Dan a curious look.

'Now that was strange. Her assistant said that she'd love to meet with me. I've got an appointment tomorrow morning, first thing.'

'With whom, exactly?'

'Clea Solana herself!'

4

A few more phone calls had established the whereabouts of both Louis Ghirardelli and Gary Krasnow. They contacted both saying only that they wanted to talk to them about Mark Zanello. Neither seemed aware of the tragic news from earlier in the day. Jilly was hoping that the news media had not gotten hold of the identification yet.

Krasnow was at work and said he would be able to meet with them later, but Ghirardelli was available right then, so Dan and Jilly drove to his apartment. He was heavy-set and friendly, with dark hair and a goatee. He only gave their badges and IDs a passing glance before inviting them in.

Stepping through the door, Jilly could immediately tell he was a single guy. He swept a pizza box and some other debris off his sofa and coffee table and invited them to sit down.

'Hope we aren't disturbing anything,' said Dan, settling himself cautiously into a mismatched recliner chair.

'Naw, nothing going on right now. I'm freelancing and work is light. So what's up that you want to talk to me about Mark? He's not in any kind of trouble, is he?'

There was a moment's silence. Dan and Jilly looked at one another and Jilly took the initiative.

'Mr. Ghirardelli, something has happened to Mark. He was found murdered this morning.'

'What? You're kidding, right? No way!' He looked back and forth at them. 'No, come on! Mark?'

'I'm sorry, sir. Yes, it's the truth.'

'Holy . . . ' He buried his face in his hands for a long moment. 'How . . . how . . . ?'

'He was apparently shot. His body was found in an abandoned building on Pilsen Avenue.'

'I don't understand. Why would he be over *there*?'

'That's what we're trying to figure out.

We're hoping you might help us. We understand you and he were close friends?'

Ghirardelli nodded. 'Oh, yeah. Yeah. We go way back. Back to Brooklyn. We went to high school together!'

'When was the last time you saw or spoke to Mark?'

He was still in shock and took a few moments for the question to sink in. 'I hadn't seen him in a couple of weeks, I'd say. He'd been busy working. I talked to him on the phone maybe a few days ago? Called him at his job. We had planned to meet up at a local club. He said he wasn't sure if he could make it. He never showed up.'

'Do you remember exactly when that was?'

Ghirardelli said blankly, 'Let's see, it would have been . . . five days ago. Friday.'

'And you and he agreed to meet up somewhere?'

'Yeah. Well, sort of. Mark was like that.' He looked up at them, refocusing. 'He was an 'OBO' kind of guy.'

'OBO?'

'As in 'or best offer,' like in the ads for selling stuff? He hated to commit to anything. All the jokes about how guys can't commit, you know? It's like, Mark *really* wouldn't pin himself down, like, to anything. He was always waiting to see if something else would come up and he'd just . . . I'm babbling, aren't I?'

'It's okay. We're following you. Go on.'

Ghirardelli kept shaking his head. 'He's really gone? Damn. I can't believe it. I'll never get to talk to him again.'

'I'm really sorry. This is hard. But whatever you can tell us might help us find out what happened.'

'Of course. Sorry. Where was I?'

'You called and you were going to meet up. Friday.'

'Yeah yeah. Told him he needed to stop working so hard, take a night off. He and I were going to go to a local watering hole, the Bucket of Blood.'

'Bucket of Blood?' said Dan. 'Really?'

'Yeah, well, it's an ironic name. Hipster bar, you know? They have bands, open microphone nights, stuff like that. Craft beers on tap.'

'Where is this place?' Jilly asked, notebook on hand.

'Right down the street. Mark doesn't live all that far from here . . . I mean he *didn't* live . . . aw, damn . . . '

'It's okay, Take your time. What time was he supposed to meet you?'

'We just kinda left it that he'd show up if he was able, like around seven or eight. I hung out and when he didn't show up, I figured, that was Mark.'

'Was anybody else with you?'

'I ran into a couple of friends, we just hung around for a while.'

'So it didn't surprise you when he didn't show up, you didn't call him or anything?'

Ghirardelli shook his head. 'Nope. That was how Mark rolls. Rolled. As long as I've known him.'

'Can you think of anybody who would have wanted to hurt him?'

He ran a hand through his mussy hair. 'No, not at all. Mark was . . . ' he stopped and got unfocused again for a moment. 'No. There's nobody.'

'Was Mark doing any kind of drugs,

involved in anything like that?' Dan asked.

'You mean, like, *drugs* drugs? No. He drank. Definitely drank. Maybe a bit too much at times. Especially lately.'

'No gambling, anything like that?' interjected Jilly. 'Anything that might have brought him into contact with a different crowd?'

'No, I mean, he followed sports and stuff, we all do. I don't think he ever bet, or like that. Once in a while we played poker. He wasn't very good. I can't see him hanging out downtown with the card players or bookies, anything like that.'

Dan nodded. 'You said especially lately he was drinking more heavily. Would that be because of his breakup with his girlfriend?'

'Oh, yeah. That just crushed him. Totally. You know about that, huh?'

'Why don't you tell us what you know about it?' Jilly said quietly, smiling kindly. 'It was hard for Mark?'

'The last few months, he was pretty crazy, getting smashed every night. Hanging out with us a lot, crying in his beer, so to speak? Then he suddenly changed, started getting really into his work, working long hours, and fell out of touch with us.'

'Excuse me, who's 'us'?'

'Oh, me and our friend Gary, Gary Krasnow. We're like, the three musketeers.'

'When did he and his girlfriend break up?'

'Let's see, that would have been — oh, wow, a good six months ago.'

'It was traumatic, you're saying?'

'Oh yeah. He found out she was sleeping with her boss. It had been going on for a while. Came as quite a shock to him.'

'How did he find out?'

'He *saw* them!' Ghirardelli shook his head and clucked his tongue. 'She had been telling him she was working late a lot. She works on this magazine. She's like the art director or designer or something like that. Said there was a chance she might get a big promotion and a nice raise so she wanted to impress the publisher. Mark was kinda excited, he figured if they had more money coming in they might finally think about getting married. Do you know what a huge thing that was for *Mark*, the OBO guy? He actually talked about it, used the M word and the whole thing!'

'But,' Dan prompted, 'he found out the truth?'

'Oh yeah. *Oh* yeah. Went out one night with a couple of the guys from his agency, which was strange, he didn't really hang out with them much, but they had just finished this major campaign thing and they invited him along and he knew she wasn't going to be home until late, so he went along. Turns out they went to this sports bar that was *right across the street* from where her boss lived. What are the odds? He saw her out the window. She was coming out of the building with him, and they were like all kissy-face and touchy-feely. The guy put her into a cab and went back into the building.'

'Ouch,' said Dan, almost reflexively.

'Exactly. Mark left and hurried home and she was already there. He let her tell him a few lies, and then he let her have it about what he saw. This had been going on for *weeks*, it turns out.'

'Couldn't have been too happy about that,' Dan said. The way he said it suggested he could relate. Jilly sat out this part of the conversation, fascinated in how Dan was gaining Ghirardelli's solidarity here.

'Oh, he was destroyed.'

'So what did he do? That night, I mean.'

'He called me up and asked if he could come over. I figured they had had a fight and she had thrown him out for the evening, I said sure, come on over.'

'Did that happen much, her throwing him out, I mean?'

'Nah. Never. Those two, they were like thick, you know?' He crossed his index and middle finger. 'Close. Real love birds. But I figured, you know, stuff happens.'

'So he came over and told you what happened. Louis, right? Can I call you Louis?'

'Sure. Louie is good, that's what they call me. Oh yeah, we got pretty loaded together. He crashed on my couch. This one right here, in fact.' He proudly gestured to the sofa on which he and Jilly were sitting. 'I had work the next day, but, you know, your bud and all, you gotta be there, Detective.'

'You can call me Dan, that's fine. Dan and Jilly. But yeah, for sure. Good thing you were there for him, I'd say. So he stayed with you after that?'

'No, she moved out. They both had kept their own places. That old *fear of commitment* thing, again, I guess.' He actually smirked, made quotation marks in the air with paired fingers. The ironic generation, Jilly thought to herself. 'She had been staying at his place but by the next day she was gone, back to her own place. She came back a few times to pick up something or to drop off something of his.'

'So that was it, they just broke off contact after that?'

'Yep, just like that.'

'So he hung with you guys, the three musketeers, a lot right after that.'

'And let me tell you, trying to keep up with him once he started hitting the drinks? A challenge, my friend. A challenge.' Louie made a pantomime of tossing back a shot several times, head tipped back.

'Mark must have been really angry.'

'Yeah, but you have to understand, Mark wasn't like a violent kind of guy. He didn't get in fights. I kinda doubt he ever even hit anybody in anger, like ever, as long as I've known him. Once or twice he, like, threw something and broke it. That was about the extent of his anger. He was more . . . sad. Really, really sad. Like, morose. Depressed.'

'He didn't say anything like he wanted to hurt this other guy?'

'Oh, sure, he said some stuff, wouldn't you? For weeks we would toast the bastard, fantasies of things we hoped would befall him, pits of poisoned stakes and stuff like that, the smug scumbag. It was all just letting off steam. In real life, I can't imagine Mark actually even considering doing honest harm to the guy.'

'Did he ever try to confront the guy?'

'No, I don't think so. Mark just decided to write her completely off. It was like she was dead to him. He wouldn't acknowledge her existence, never mentioned her after a while. It was like those Orthodox Jewish guys who ostracize a family member and declare them dead?'

'I've heard of that. In some extreme cases, someone might say the prayers for the dead for them. Real finality. That's a pretty serious resentment.'

'Yeah, well, Mark wasn't Orthodox, he wasn't even Jewish, though being from Brooklyn, we were familiar with that culture. I'm just using that as an example of how serious he was about forgetting she existed.'

'So he cut off all communication with her, never tried to contact anyone she knew, not the new boyfriend, nobody?'

Louie shook his head. 'Not that I ever knew of. And at that time we were spending a lot of time together, him and me and Gary.'

'Do you happen to know the name of the boss, or the name of the place she worked?'

'Oh, let me think, His girlfriend's name was Kerry. I mean, it still is, she's just not his girlfriend anymore. Oh damn, of course she isn't. I'm sorry.' He started shaking his head vigorously and grimacing.

'It's all right, you're doing fine.'

'Kerry Moran. She works for . . . it's a hip magazine, they publish a paper edition and they're also online . . . *On The Spot*. I used to pick it up on occasion. I guess I felt I had to stop out of loyalty.'

'And the guy, her boss?'

'I don't know, I heard Mark mention his name here and there. Kevin something. He used to make comments about '*Kev-innn.*' Or more usually, '*Freak-inggg Kev-inn.*' Or, you know, worse. Especially when he got sloshed.'

'So you say he was drinking heavily. Did he lose his job?'

'No, his own boss was totally cool about it. He told Mark to take some time off, not to take *too* long but to come back when he felt better. I mean, I'm sure the guy had a limit, but he was cool. They were really supportive of Mark.'

'Do you know his boss's name,

anything about the agency where he worked?'

'Yeah, it's called *Burnt Toast*. Young, hip, up and coming. The guy who runs it is named Jamie Farad.'

Jilly noted the name in her book. She observed that Dan had made no effort to take notes but was totally concentrating on Louie.

'Louie, I gotta say, Mark sounds like he showed remarkable self-control. I mean, I've been in that kind of a situation, not exactly like that but close enough. And I tell you, I'd have been all over that other guy at some point.'

Louie nodded gravely. 'It occurred to me, but that's just not Mark, that's just not how he rolled.'

'So he finally straightened up and quit drinking and returned to work? How long ago was that?'

'Oh, maybe three months or so now. That's when we stopped seeing him very much.'

'His job was there, waiting for him.'

'Yeah. In fact I think Jamie gave him a raise or some kind of incentive.'

'He felt like he needed to throw himself into his work.'

'There you go. He needed the distraction and he must have felt like he owed them for treating him so well.'

'So work became pretty much his whole life for the past few months.'

'Yeah, I guess so. If there was anything else going on, he didn't talk to me or Gary about it.'

'So you wouldn't have known if, say, he had decided to go look up this other guy, this Kevin, maybe have it out with him.'

'I tell you, I sincerely doubt he would have done that. He wanted that stuff behind him.'

'Do you know anything about what might have happened with his girlfriend, Kerry?'

Louie shrugged. 'No idea. I assume she's still shacked up with *Kev*-in. Maybe she's gonna marry *him*. I don't really care about that witch.'

'Is there anything you can do here, to help shed light on this thing for us, Louie? He got killed in a really bad part of town you said he never went to, he didn't associate with drug dealers or gamblers or gangsters, you say he wouldn't have gone looking for a fight with anybody. So . . . ' Dan shook his hands in the air in frustration. 'Can you think of *any* reason this would have happened where it did?'

Louie thought for a long moment, his head slowly shaking. 'Only thing I can think of, it's a long shot. But it's absolutely the only thing I can think of.'

'Yeah, tell me, I'm desperate here, Louie. Tell us.'

'The magazine,' he said. 'They did articles on gang life, stuff like that.'

'Recently?'

'Within the last year or so. They did a few features on the Roland 29s and the Brown Skulls or whatever they're called. Aren't they from down that area?'

Dan nodded. 'More or less.'

'Like I said, it's kind of a stretch, but it was while Mark and Kerry were still together, maybe he was down at the offices and met one of those guys when they were being interviewed. It's the only thing I can think of.'

Dan and Jilly exchanged a look.

'Let me ask you something else,' Jilly interjected. 'If Mark had been going to meet you the other night — you said four days ago? — at the . . . Bucket of Blood?' She said the name as if it were a tangible object she was trying to avoid touching.

'Yeah?'

'You said it was close to both of you. Would he have driven there, or would he have walked?'

'Mark wasn't much of a walker. I woulda thought he'd drive. It would've been about an eight block walk from his place. I think he'd still have wanted to drive.'

'And where does he usually park his car around his apartment?'

'On the street. There's no parking garage or lot or anything where he is. In fact it's a pain in the neck because there's street cleaning and you have to move your car two days a week or get a ticket.'

There wasn't much more after that. They thanked him, left cards, and moved on.

* * *

'Nice job in there,' Jilly said as they walked back to her car.

'Not that we got all that much from him,' Dan replied.

'Yeah, but you got him to open up. I don't know, he just struck me as kind of a loser. That might have come through. I might not have related to him quite that effectively. It was a help, in any case.'

Dan made a wry face. 'I guess I relate to losers better than you.'

'Oh come on, I didn't ... ' Jilly stopped as she saw Dan break into a broad smile.

'Actually, this Mark himself strikes me as kind of a loser, you know? At the very least, he was a really private guy. Not too many friends, seems as if he was kinda passive.'

'Played his cards close to the vest, as they used to say,' said Jilly. 'A definite enigma.'

'So I'm thinking the agency is next?' Dan said. 'Last people to spend quality time with the deceased.'

'Agreed,' replied Jilly. 'We can talk to Kerry's old boss once we've got a handle on Mark's recent state of mind.'

'Save the best for last,' Dan said wryly.

5

Burnt Toast was the kind of young boutique agency that they expected. It occupied a reception area and two large open areas in a recently renovated building, with trendy interior decor: exposed pipes and beams, high ceilings, minimal furnishings. About ten employees, all twenty-somethings, occupied plain glass and enamel desks scattered at the peripheries of the space. Computer monitors were everywhere.

It was like an anthill: everyone animated, constantly talking, moving about, energy everywhere. Sounds echoed in the large spaces. Jamie Farad, the owner, was the sole person with a private office. He came out to greet them with a smile and an extended hand. He looked to be slightly older than his staff, with closely-buzzed hair, a fashionable goatee, black shirt and slacks.

'Detectives,' he said. 'How may I help

105

you? This is about Mark, I understand?'

'That's right, Mr. Farad, may we talk in your office?'

'Jamie, please,' he said, his smile starting to turn more serious as he observed their own demeanor. 'Sure, come right in.

They were seated in front of Farad's large glass desk and he settled into his own comfortable chair. Now he looked concerned. 'Mark hasn't been in now for a few days. We haven't been able to get hold of him. Is he all right?'

'No, I'm afraid not,' Jilly said. 'He was killed. His body was found this morning.'

'Oh my God,' Farad mumbled, looking genuinely shocked. 'No.'

'I'm sorry we have to be the ones to let you know this way. But we're hoping you might be of some help to us in our investigation.'

'Of course,' Farad nodded earnestly. 'Of course. What happened to him?'

'We're not really sure. He was found in a deserted building on Pilsen Avenue. He had been shot.'

'Pilsen? What was he doing over there?'

'We don't know yet.'

'That's a sketchy neighborhood, very sketchy. I wouldn't walk there any time of day.'

'So you can't think of any reason he might have been there?'

Farad thought, shook his head. 'No, not at all.'

'It would seem that you and the people here were the only ones with whom Mark had any contact in recent days,' Jilly continued.

'I wouldn't be surprised. Mark was a rather private sort of person. Very intense, very guarded. He'd had some difficult times recently and I think he was throwing himself into his work just to get past them. He certainly was spending a lot of time here in the studios. I can't believe that this has happened to him. This is terrible. You say he was shot?'

'Yes. Apparently at close range.

'A robbery maybe? Mugging? Carjacking? This could not have been someone who he knew.'

'Nobody you could think of, then?' asked Dan.

'No. Absolutely not.'

'No clients from that neck of the woods? Redevelopment agencies, charities, pro bono work?'

'We have a very high-end high-profile kind of clientele,' Farad said. 'Digital tech, luxury commerce, cutting edge technology. Nobody from the other side of Twentieth Street. I don't mean to sound snobbish, believe me. It's just that's who we work with.'

'So when was the last time you saw Mark?'

Farad sat back in his chair and thought. Jilly noted that he was the sort of measured person who tended to think before he spoke. 'That would have been end of last week. Friday. He hasn't been in to work all week.'

'Did anybody try to go over to see him at home or anything like that?'

'No, we just kept leaving him calls. He never picked up.'

'Nobody was concerned enough to report him missing?'

'Well, as I said, Mark recently had some personal troubles and kind of dropped out. I thought perhaps he had had a relapse, so to speak. I was willing to cut him some slack, a few days to sort out whatever he was still going through. By next week I would have been more concerned.

'Although it did bother me that he hadn't tried to get in touch with me. He was straight up with me about what was going on from the beginning. It was unlike him to just suddenly not show up. But as I say, I was willing to give him some benefit of the doubt.'

Jilly and Dan didn't immediately answer so he continued. 'Mark has always been a good guy here. He's a valued worker. Highly valued. He's a big reason a few of our recent campaigns have been so successful. I've been willing to go to the mat for him and I've never regretted it.'

'What was his state of mind like the past few weeks?' Jilly asked.

'He seemed to be getting his groove back. He actually was smiling, even telling jokes. He seemed more alert. I think he had given up the drinking.'

'I understand you gave him some time off when he first had his personal problems,' Jilly said. 'You were quite generous and patient with him.'

Farad waved a hand. 'I valued Mark very highly here. He had the emotional and psychic equivalent of a ton of bricks dropped upon him out of nowhere . . .'

'Yes,' interrupted Jilly, 'the girlfriend. The other man.'

Farad nodded. 'You have to understand something, Detective. Mark is — I mean *was*, this is so hard to get my head around. He *was* extremely focused, almost tunnel-visioned. It was why he was so good at what he did here. But not when it came to his girlfriend Kerry. She was the only human being who had been able to pierce through that single-mindedness. Oh, Mark was a very likable guy, don't get me wrong, but he was all work. Except where she was concerned. So naturally he took this hard. Insanely hard. I felt my best course of action was to let him go do whatever it was he needed to do, work it out and then when he was ready to come back, he was welcome to do so.'

'And how long did that take?'

'I'd say about ten or twelve weeks altogether? To be honest, I was beginning to get a little concerned that perhaps he wasn't *coming* back. Then one day he called and said he was ready. Just like that.'

'And you had no contact with him in that time he was away?'

'None. What I heard was that he was deeply depressed. Drinking heavily.' He shrugged, continuing to carefully choose his words. 'I don't know of any other substances being involved, if that's a concern.'

'And when he came back?' Dan asked.

'He was straight as an arrow. Sober. Serious. Focused. And he stayed that way.'

'How did he get along with everyone here?' Dan continued. 'Any difficulties?'

Farad shook his head, looking almost amused at the thought. 'Mark was easy to get along with. He was an odd combination, aloof but friendly, rather passive, highly focused on his job, but never difficult, no ego to speak of. He never even had arguments. He had opinions and ideas and we all took them seriously, but he was always willing to work towards a consensus. He was the perfect guy for this job, do you know? A people person of an odd sort, but without too strong or abrasive a personality.'

Jilly moved on. 'What did he do here?'

'We don't have traditional job descriptions as such here. We expect a lot of cross-discipline thinking. Well, except for the really specialized work like the graphics.' Farad juggled his hands up and down. 'Mark was sort of like what you'd have called an account executive, mixed with a concept man, mixed with a copywriter.'

'I see,' mumbled Dan, not really seeing all that well.

'And a few other things thrown in as well.' Farad laughed. 'We all make the coffee and doughnut runs too.'

'Did he have a title?' Jilly asked.

'No, on his business card it simply said, 'Idea Team.' That's what all of our cards generally say.'

'I bet yours is a bit more specific,' Jilly said.

Farad shrugged. 'I've got five separate cards, Detective, depending upon who I need to be talking to. That's the *Burnt Toast* way, we're very holistic here.'

'But getting back to Mark,' continued Jilly. 'The breakup with his girlfriend. Did he talk about her or about that whole thing much when he was back at work?'

'Not that I'm aware of,' Farad said, stroking his goatee with thumb and forefinger. 'But I'm often in here, by necessity, while the real action is going on out there in the trenches. You'll definitely want to talk to some of the other team members.'

'We'd appreciate that, thank you.'

'Of course,' Farad nodded earnestly. 'They're all going to need to know this sad information as well.'

They continued the conversation with Farad for a few more minutes before moving on to Mark's co-workers. He led them out of his office into the adjoining workspace and called for everyone's attention.

Not surprisingly, there was general dismay over the news of Mark's death. There were some general remarks made by Dan and Jilly before Farad excused himself, shaking each of their hands and saying, 'Please let me know if you need anything else of me while you're here or any time. I hope you find the persons who did this.'

Within a few minutes they had ascertained that Mark seemed to have been respected and liked by everyone but had really been at all close to only three people working in the agency. They pulled them aside to have a further conversation.

There were two young men, Pablo and Sam, and a young woman, Janice (which she pronounced 'Janeese'). They were all identically dressed in black tee shirts and skinny jeans, the two men both had carefully stubbly chin hair, and Sam and Janice wore big glasses with heavy black rims. It quickly became clear that once Mark had returned to work, he had been all business. He no longer joined any of his co-workers after work to socialize. He worked long hours and talked about little else except for work. He was personable and agreeable, but it had become clear that he needed to think of nothing but work.

None of them had seen Mark take a drink since the ill-fated night he had discovered Kerry with her boss: in fact that had been in the company of Pablo and Sam.

'How did you three happen to become his closest associates here at work?' asked Jilly.

They bobbed heads back and forth at one another before Janice spoke up. 'Maybe it was because we all worked together on a few accounts and we all seemed to jibe well. Similar ideas but different. Synergies.' The two men nodded vigorously at that.

'So, no arguments, no fights, with anyone here? Everyone played nice together, is that what you're telling us?'

Janice continued, speaking animatedly. 'Oh, it gets pretty intense working around here, believe me, there are fights, people blowing off steam. Of course there are. We work long hours in close vicinity to one another, we keep up the energy, we guzzle caffeine and energy drinks all day, we bounce off each other, we get crazy.'

She shook her head and her dark ponytail and dangly earrings wagged back and forth, her eyes huge behind the glasses. 'But not Mark. Nobody ever had problems with Mark. I don't ever remember him getting into it with anyone here, not ever. He always backed off, always found a way to be diplomatic and accommodating.'

Sam and Pablo first shook their heads and then nodded, both in agreement with her.

Jilly was beginning to feel like she was looking at a shelf of bobbleheads wagging up and down and side to side. She shot a sideways glance at Dan, who shot one back at her. Synergy indeed.

★ ★ ★

They were walking back to the car, still shaking their heads at the encounter with the Idea Team. 'So what we seem to have here,' Jilly said to Dan, 'is a kind of self-absorbed, passive guy who didn't start fights, kept his feelings to himself, and was re-directing all of his energies into work. Downright ascetic. Hardly the kind of guy who would go out looking for a violent confrontation, if you can believe what we're hearing.'

'Those psychology courses really paid off, huh?' Dan replied with a smile. 'Of course, there's the possibility that he really wasn't re-directing all the anger and resentment and stuff. Maybe he was just bottling it up and one day it exploded.'

'Sounds like you took a few of those courses yourself, partner.'

'And then maybe everybody's not telling the truth.'

'All those sincerely bobbing heads? How can you doubt them?'

Dan rolled his eyes. 'And yet somehow it doesn't feel right that one of them is hiding something about Mark.'

'Yeah, I'm of a similar mind.' Jilly was increasingly finding that she and her new partner apparently had similar instincts. That was all to the good.

'So are you thinking what I'm thinking?'

'Time to go talk to Kerry's boss,' Jilly nodded, looking at her watch. 'We got a while before we can see Gary Krasnow yet anyway. I have a feeling he's just going to tell us what everybody else has been saying. There doesn't seem to be a break here for us at all.'

'The boss,' agreed Dan. 'It's looking better and better. If that's the right word for it.'

★   ★   ★

A small suite of offices in a fashionably historic building housed *On The Spot*. The magazine was a trendy, oversized, overly expensive slick monthly that was sold in hip coffeehouses and what remained of bookstores and newsstands. The online Internet edition was increasingly becoming the more popular alternative. They were both able to familiarize themselves further by perusing back copies in the reception area as they waited to speak to publisher Kevin

118

Warfield. Neither of them were all that impressed. It was oriented to an audience in their twenties or early thirties and featured splashy graphics and pithy features on popular culture, fashion, and current events. In some ways it more closely resembled a giveaway tabloid newspaper, the kind one found in newspaper dispensers in most large cities, except that this one cost thirty-five dollars an issue. Jilly found it all rather shallow, self-conscious and overly clever. She decided the writers were trying to present 'think pieces' in the style of more established magazines she herself had long enjoyed reading, but they lacked the depth to do it effectively.

The magazine was, she had to admit, ambitious in its scope. It regularly ran feature articles by currently hot writers and media personalities and series attempting to be 'hard hitting' and 'socially relevant'.

Leafing through a number of back issues only made Jilly feel old beyond her years.

Kevin Warfield greeted them in the reception area, looking very much like a traditional publisher — vest, shirtsleeves, expensive tie. He shook their hands and led them back through a labyrinth of cubicles, filled with the sounds of journalists at work: voices loud and soft, phones buzzing in odd tones, keyboards and monitors making distinctive keyboard and monitor noises.

The workspaces were utilitarian and cluttered. Graphics filled every wall space: photos, posters, artwork. Warfield had the corner office overlooking a busy intersection. He motioned them to chairs and sat down behind his desk.

'Detectives, how may I help you?' he said brusquely. He was perhaps in his forties, rather ruggedly handsome, well groomed, with a full head of dark brown hair with just a touch of grey at the temples. He looked as if he worked out and paid attention to his health.

'You had an employee working here until fairly recently, I believe she was your art director, Kerry Moran?' Jilly said. That provoked a deep sigh in Warfield.

'Yes. What is this, has she filed some complaint against me or something of the sort? I kind of expected she might do that but it's been a while now and I thought . . . '

'No, sir, she hasn't filed a complaint against you as yet,' Dan interrupted. 'Not that we're aware, at any rate. Did you know her former boyfriend, Mark Zanello, by any chance?'

Warfield stared at them. 'I heard of him, yes. Never met him in person. Couldn't even tell you what he looks like. And this is about what, now?'

Jilly brought up the photo of Mark on her phone and placed it on the desk in front of him. 'You've never seen this man, are you positive?'

Warfield looked down at the picture for several seconds, then back up at her. 'I've never seen this man before in my life. This looks like he's dead. Is that what you're telling me?'

Jilly took back her phone. 'Yes, that is what I'm telling you. You don't know him, you've never encountered him?'

Warfield shook his head, looking a bit surprised. 'Absolutely not. What happened? What is this all about?'

'He was found murdered this morning.'

'And that's Kerry's boyfriend?'

'He was, up until a few months ago. Mr. Warfield, it's our understanding you had a relationship with Kerry Moran while she was in your employ?'

'Good Lord, you don't think I had anything to do with this?'

Jilly and Dan waited.

'A relationship,' Warfield shook his head with a wry smile. 'Is that what she told you?'

'We're interested in what you have to tell us, actually,' said Dan.

Warfield sat back in his chair and took another deep sigh before answering. 'Yes, you could say that. She and I had a *relationship*. We spent some time together.'

'You knew she was in a serious relationship with Mark? That they were engaged to be married?'

'She had mentioned that, yes,' he said matter-of-factly.

'Apparently *that* relationship had some problems. She was very interested in spending time with me, you might say. We would hang out after work, go to lunch, things like that. She liked to talk to me, confide in me. Things just sort of happened.'

'You had an affair,' Jilly suggested.

Warfield shrugged, raised his hands. 'Call it what you will. I think she took it quite a bit more seriously than I did.'

'Mr. Warfield, you're married?'

'Yes. Yes, I am.'

'Did Kerry know that?'

'I let her know. I was honest with her.'

'Were you aware that Mark found out about the two of you?'

'I heard about that, yes.'

'Was that before or after you informed her you were married?'

'Look, what is this all about?'

'Were you aware that when Mark discovered you two were having your affair . . . '

'Whoa, wait a minute, You're using the word 'affair,' not me.'

' . . . When Mark learned about the two of you, he left her? Were you aware of that?'

Warfield nodded. 'Sure. She told me.'

'And that's when you developed a concern about your own relationship with her and told her you were married?'

'I don't remember the exact sequence of events, Detective. And I'm not sure I like where this is going.'

'Kerry was your art director for some time, wasn't she?'

'Yes, more than a year.'

'And yet you suddenly decided to fire her?'

'Her work declined. She was distracted. I saw that developing for some time, had addressed that with her on a number of occasions. I documented our discussions as well.'

'Up until then, was she a good art director?'

'She started out an excellent designer and art director. Great ideas. Made the whole look of the magazine what it was. I had high hopes for her. I thought she had a great future with us. I considered creating a new executive level post of creative director, branching out into more publications and other ventures. Then everything started going south with her.'

It was Jilly's turn to take a deep breath and gather her thoughts before continuing. Dan watched her with interest.

'So, let me see, she enters into an intimate relationship with you — is that term acceptable? — which results in the termination of her own long-term relationship with Mark Zanello and apparently a good deal of emotional turmoil for her, immediately after which you inform her you're married, terminate the relationship you two have been pursuing, and then dismiss her shortly thereafter? Would I have this timeline correct, Mr. Warfield?'

He leaned forward, stared at them both earnestly, spoke quietly but insistently. 'Her view of our relationship, as you put it, was clearly different from my own. We had several conversations in which I attempted to clarify that, definitely. She was being unrealistic. If you've spoken with her, perhaps you understand what I'm talking about. Kerry is a lovely girl, very sweet, very intelligent, but with a naive romantic streak. She's looking for some kind of storybook existence that's just never going to happen. I didn't want to hurt her feelings. I only wanted her to be realistic.'

'Were you ever aware of how Mark reacted to all of this?' Jilly asked.

'Well, Kerry told me, of course, but I never heard anything from Mark himself. As I said, I never had any contact with him.'

Dan had picked up an older copy of the magazine that was sitting on a side table and was leafing through it, noting the cover story. 'You did a feature on youth gangs of the city a while back?'

Warfield seemed taken aback by this sudden change in subject. 'Why, yes. About a year ago. We interviewed a few young men from various cliques and sets.'

Dan held up the issue, that featured a stylized photo of a young man in a denim jacket over a dark hoodie, scowling to the side as he walked down an urban street. 'Like the Roland 29s?'

'Sure, we did the Roland 29s. And Drew Road. And the Brown Street Skulls. Why?'

'Did you get to meet any of the gang members, I mean you yourself?'

Now he looked truly mystified, shaking his head very slightly. 'No, that was a series by one of our reporters. Two, actually, a man and a woman. Great pieces, very sensitive and insightful. I saw them, of course, the editor runs everything by me. We had hopes the series would have social impact in the city. But I wasn't personally involved in any of the stories, no. Why?'

'Just curious,' Dan shrugged, putting the magazine back down. 'So you don't know anyone who might be a member of the 29s?'

'Of course not.' He said it as if Dan had suggested something beyond belief. So much, Dan thought, for the journalistic social crusader. A slick trendy magazine didn't really lend itself to gritty muck raking, it would get the suit smudged. 'What's your point? What's that got to do with what we're talking about?'

Jilly picked up again, finding a new appreciation in how Dan was working off of her to keep him off balance. 'I still want to understand how you viewed this intimate relationship with Kerry. You really didn't find it very serious at all?'

'I liked her very much. She's a very sweet girl. She's got a wonderful energy for life. She's quirkily attractive, she's got a vulnerability and a real charm to her. Sure I was taken by her. As I said, things just happened. But she interpreted what had happened the wrong way. And then it began to affect everything in her life.'

'So her entire life got upturned in the matter of a few days, maybe. It pretty much got destroyed, both hers and Mark's. And you just washed your hands of the whole thing?' Jilly opened her eyes wide, gestured with her hands, and having dropped the ball back into his court, just stared at Warfield. There was a long awkward silence.

'You can see our point of view, can't you,' Dan finally interjected, 'why we might be a little confused here? That Mark never tried to contact you, never talked to you? Maybe you can help us out here a little? Maybe he *tried* to contact you, came to the office, and the receptionist wouldn't let him in? Maybe you left word to not allow him in?'

Warfield shook his head, his stare becoming a glare. 'I did no such thing. I wouldn't have tried to run or hide from anyone. Kerry never returned, this Mark never approached me. Not here at work, not out of work, nowhere, at no time.'

Jilly and Dan continued their efforts for a while longer but the conversation continued in much the same vein. Warfield continued to insist he had never seen or met Mark Zanello, that he had had no contact whatsoever with Kerry's world since dismissing her.

Finally Jilly and Dan each handed him a card and suggested that if he were to think of anything that might be of help, to contact them.

As they rose, Warfield asked, 'Can you tell me how Mark Zanello died, the circumstances?'

'He was shot at close range,' Dan said straight-faced. 'And his body was hidden in a deserted building.'

'My lord,' Warfield muttered. 'How

horrible. How bizarre. And you have no clues, no leads?'

'We didn't say that,' retorted Jilly.

'Well, I certainly hope you find out who did this to him. Of course.' He paused for a minute. 'Perhaps the magazine can be of some help. Can I have one of our reporters contact you?'

Jilly considered several replies but finally just shrugged silently as they turned to leave.

A brief conversation with the receptionist confirmed that she had no recollection of Mark Zanello, or anyone meeting his description, ever coming to the offices or trying to contact Warfield. They left the offices and took the stairs down the two flights to the street level.

Jilly exhaled loudly as they descended. 'What a slimebag.'

'Yeah,' Dan agreed. He looked at Jilly. 'Do women really find that guy attractive? I mean, did you?'

'Well, he's rugged, well built, he's kind of worldly, clearly got some money, he's mature — a little bit of a father figure maybe. I could see a certain kind of gal would go for him.'

Dan considered that, tilting his head back and forth.

'Totally messed that girl's life up. I wanted to ask him how his marriage is doing but I thought that might not be all that appropriate.'

'I'd be very surprised if the affair was an isolated incident,' Dan agreed. 'Quite a few attractive young women working up there.'

'You noticed,' Jilly smirked. Dan just pursed his lips and said nothing more.

'No responsibility for what he's done. Wonder if he's hired any new young ingénue types in the meantime to replace Kerry, in more ways than one. Yeah, a slimebag.'

'But,' Dan replied, 'I'm not getting feelings that he's good for the murder, are you?'

'No,' Jilly sighed deeply as they reached the bottom of the stairwell. Kevin Warfield was guilty, but not of what they wanted him to be. 'No, I'm not either.'

'Long day,' Jilly murmured as she pulled out her cell phone one more time.

'Let's talk to this Gary Krasnow and get ourselves back to the station. Maybe there'll be some good news.'

'Why do I have the feeling,' said Dan, 'that this guy is going to tell us exactly the same thing that everybody else did about Mark Zanello?'

Dan turned out to be absolutely right.

Krasnow told her he was able to get out of work early and would be glad to meet them at his apartment. He gave her an address and said he'd be there within the half hour. The conversation was quick and seemed like a rerun of their earlier one with Louis Ghirardelli. Krasnow was also shocked at the news of Mark's death, asked a few questions as to the circumstances, and then asked how he could be of help to their investigation.

He was a pleasant enough fellow, energetic and intelligent. He joked that he was the only one of the 'three musketeers' who held down a 'normal' job, in an insurance agency. Some years back he had met Mark when his sister briefly dated him — nothing that ever developed seriously, he said — and while that couple had not worked out, he and Mark had become friends. He befriended Mark's boyhood pal Louie as well, and the 'three musketeers' had formed.

The portrait he drew of Mark was similar to that of everyone else with whom they had spoken that day: introspective, reticent, focused to the point of distraction. He told the identical story about the disintegration of Mark's relationship with Kerry, his tailspin into heavy drinking, and his apparent resurrection.

Krasnow had not been in contact with Mark since his return to work with a single-minded vengeance. He could not even begin to account for the hows and whys of Mark's murder. It was as mystifying to him as to everyone else.

★ ★ ★

'There's nothing,' Jilly muttered as they drove back to the station. 'Unless this guy just stepped into the wrong place at the wrong time and got randomly killed.'

'Yeah,' said Dan. 'Against the odds, but

133

if it turned out to be true, we might never find out what happened.' Random events were a concept they both hated to accept. It did happen on rare occasion, but all their training and instinct went against it. There was almost always a pattern, a logic. They just had to find it.

'There is one other possible explanation though,' Jilly said reluctantly. 'That somehow this all really is related to Kerry and the Dane Spilwell case.'

★   ★   ★

A large part of every law enforcement officer's day is taken up with the prosaic and mind-deadening pursuit of paper. There are reports to be filled, documentation to establish, every 'I' to be dotted and 't' to be crossed in the interest of future prosecutions and court procedures, lest a promising case be scuttled by a technical misstep. Dan and Jilly would be spending time at the squad room filling out their own documentation of their interviews. And the techs who had investigated the crime scene that morning would be busy filling out their own as well.

Jilly was happily surprised to find the preliminary reports already on her desk when they returned. She scanned them quickly.

'Two slugs, 38 caliber revolver,' she read. 'Time of death estimated at five days ago, Friday evening.' She flipped a page. 'Evidence consistent with his being dragged into the building after being shot. Not much luck with fingerprints, there's too much 'noise' everywhere. No clear footprints on the floor. The homeless couple likely covered up anything that might have remained from the killer.'

'What are the odds on our finding the weapon?' asked Dan. 'Not great.'

'We have to hope for a break on that.'

'Let's see what tomorrow brings. So you'll be hobnobbing with the jet set.'

'Yeah, that's going to be interesting. Clea Solana herself. I wonder why she's so eager to talk to me.'

'I guess you're going to find out.'

6

Clea and Giovanni Solana, when they happened to be in the vicinity, resided in an elite gated community high in the affluent hills to the east of the city. On a day less rainy and cloud-obscured, there would have been a magnificent sweeping view of the coast and the sea to the west.

Their home was an elegantly under-stated villa in an Italian architectural style. Jilly had to admit feeling self-conscious about meeting with such a high-profile celebrity in a rather intimidating setting. She had quietly scolded herself the entire morning as she drove to the meeting, reminding herself that an effective police officer needed to maintain confidence and control.

She wore one of the suits she usually reserved for court appearances, where the proper gravitas needed to be projected. Reggie had liked to kid her about her 'power suits', and she would respond by pointing out his own partiality to expensive pinstriped three-piece suits. Soon the 'power suit' joke had become a standard with Reg and Red, being bandied back and forth between them regularly. She smiled at the memories of her partner, distracted from her self-consciousness.

The door was answered by a smiling staffer who obviously had expected her. She was instantly invited into a large hallway and escorted through several large rooms into a comfortable study, slightly sunken, with thick carpeting and soft couches and chairs.

'Ms. Solana will be right with you,' smiled the assistant, a dark-haired young woman with a soft Italian accent. Sure enough, mere moments after she had departed and Jilly had settled into one of the chairs, Clea Solana herself was descending the three steps from the entryway as if she were the Sun Queen herself.

She had a long lush mane of hair and wore an expensive silk pantsuit and just a touch of jewelry. Someone fond of clichés might have said her smile lit up the room.

But what immediately struck Jilly was exactly what she had anticipated with some dread. Surrounded by all the style and beauty her wealth and breeding could afford, her face was still irremediably disfigured. Her lips were swollen and her skin was alternately scarred, creased, and smooth-textured like a plastic doll's. The effect was bizarre.

Jilly had of course prepared herself for this meeting, having read and heard much of Clea's history. She was an intelligent, talented, and cultured woman from a celebrated international family, but somehow that had never been enough, even after marrying the successful producer-director Giovanni Solana and successfully making her own mark in numerous artistic endeavors.

Possibly to overcome some insecurity, she had sought out plastic surgeons all over the world to make her beautiful. Things had somehow gone all wrong.

Chief among those failed surgeons, Jilly reflected, was Dane Spilwell.

All of this flew through her head in a

split second and she hoped she had not shown her hesitation. She rose from the chair to greet Clea.

'Detective Garvey? I am Clea Solana. How very nice of you to come visit. Welcome!' Her smile was huge, her manner gracious and inviting, and she acted as if she was indeed the stunning beauty she had tried so hard to become. Somehow she made Jilly relax and feel more comfortable.

So much, Jilly mused to herself, for the police officer taking control of every situation.

'Please, have a seat, let me get us something. Would you prefer coffee, tea?'

'Coffee would be wonderful, thank you,' Jilly replied. She noted that another staffer had already mysteriously materialized alongside Clea and was nodding at her directions. Clea spoke softly and courteously to the young woman and in moments she was gone again.

Clea even sat elegantly, with almost regal bearing. She crossed her legs gracefully and turned her attention to Jilly. Her own voice also bore a lilting northern Italian accent. 'I am delighted to have the chance to meet you in person.'

'Thank you for having me, Ms. Solana. I have to admit, I was surprised to get such an eager reception when I called.'

Clea nodded with a serious frown. 'I left word that if you were to try to reach me while I'm still here in your lovely city, you were to be given an immediate appointment. I received word that someone had recently tried to communicate with me about the recent trial. Unfortunately the person who took the call didn't handle it well, simply told me it was a woman. I thought it might have been you, and so I made sure our staff was prepared, should you call back.'

'That actually wasn't me, but I'm aware of what happened, and it does have some bearing on why I'm here now.'

'I followed the trial as carefully as I could. You know, traveling and all, it is not always easy. Laura Spilwell was a dear friend of mine. Her death was a horrible tragedy.'

Jilly leaned forward. This was unexpected. Clea Solana had never figured in the trial and she had had no idea that the two women had even met, much less had ever been close.

'I was fascinated by the testimony and the news articles throughout the case about you and your partner, Detective Martinez, I believe?'

'Yes, Reginald Martinez.'

'And how is he? I would have loved to meet you both.'

'Unfortunately,' Jilly said, 'Detective Martinez passed away earlier this year.'

'Oh no! I had no idea! Please, forgive me!' She seemed genuinely disturbed that she had not known of Reggie's death. 'It's the travel, so many things constantly . . . '

'Perfectly all right, Ms. Solana.'

'May I ask, what happened? He was such a handsome man, so . . . strong, so intelligent, always impeccably dressed. Such a favorable impression he always gave!'

Yeah, that was Reggie. 'He was killed in the line of duty. He was part of a police action, a raid on a house where two fugitives were in hiding. Gunfire was exchanged. He died in the hospital a day later.'

'How horrible! Did he have a family?'

'Yes, a wife and two children. A son and a daughter.'

Clea actually rose and walked over to sit next to Jilly and took her hands. 'I am so, so sorry. What a terrible loss.'

Jilly nodded and smiled, looking down at the entwined hands. 'Yes, it was. He was an excellent detective. Great partner. Good friend. And a good man.'

'When, if I might ask, did this happen?'

'It was not quite four months ago.'

Two young attendants — somehow their personal bearing made it difficult for Jilly to think of them as servants — entered the room and set up a side table with cups and an actual espresso machine, as well as a tray of what looked like small pastries. It was a perfect moment to change the mood of the conversation.

'I hope good strong espresso is to your liking?' Clea brightened.

'That sounds absolutely fantastic,' Jilly admitted.

Serving out of the way, the conversation resumed. Clea sat back but remained in close proximity to Jilly as if they had established some secret intimacy between themselves.

'So now, please, tell me how I may help you?'

'Well, I suppose my main objective was to make sure that the person who tried to contact you hadn't caused any . . . problems of any sort.'

Clea seemed amused. 'Not at all. As I said, unfortunately I was never even informed when she tried to talk to me. May I ask what this was all about?'

'It was a young woman with very good intentions but, well, interfering with police matters. We were concerned that she might have given the wrong impression that she represented legitimate authorities, that sort of thing.'

Clea nodded, thoughtful. 'The trial is over. Dane Spilwell was found guilty, was he not?'

'Yes he was.'

'I was amazed by everything that happened. It was such a shock to find out that Laura had died, and just how it had occurred. And it was a surprise to learn that her husband had committed the crime.'

'A surprise?'

'Oh, I had no doubt he did it. You were clearly extremely competent detectives, I could see, two of the best. If you were confident in the evidence, I was convinced, and very early on in the case.'

'It sounds as if you followed the whole thing very carefully, then.'

'As close as I could, given my crazy schedule, mine and Giovanni's. We do try to spend some time together despite our demanding businesses. But yes. As I said, Laura was very dear to me.'

'Forgive me,' Jilly said carefully, 'but I was unaware that you and Laura Spilwell had been so close.'

'And of course that interests you. I'm glad to tell you about it. You probably know that Dane Spilwell performed surgeries upon me a few years ago.' She stared directly into Jilly's face, as if defying her to stare back. Jilly held the gaze of that oddly misshapen face. 'Detective, when I was younger, I was foolish, I was very, *very* foolish. I grew up in a milieu of beauty and style and appearance and I believed that those were the important things to life. I was so very unhappy with what I saw when I looked in the mirror. My parents, my family, my various boyfriends and lovers, all tried to reassure me that they found me beautiful, but I could not believe any of them. What I saw was not beautiful. I don't know if you can understand how one can look into the mirror and see only what they shouldn't see.'

'Many young women do exactly that,' Jilly said.

'Sadly, yes. We can be smart, we can be perceptive, we can be loved and secure, and we still see ourselves as unattractive. We can fear losing those we love and cherish unless we become more attractive. And so, I tried to do that. My family had the resources. I consulted with surgeons around the world. I ignored their advice against many of the things I insisted be done. And well . . . ' Clea raised her eyebrows and extended her hands out . . . 'when there is considerable money involved, people begin to tell you what you wish to hear, they begin to do inadvisable things because you insist upon them.'

Clea raised her head high. 'And this is now what I live with. The woman in the mirror is still not what I wish. In many ways, ironically, nothing has really changed in that regard. What has changed is that I recognize that the people who love me and care about me, who have stayed with me. They are what make me beautiful. Or ugly.'

Jilly simply nodded.

'My last surgeries were with Dane Spilwell,' Clea continued. 'We came here. That is when we bought this lovely villa, in fact. He is a brilliant surgeon, and he came with excellent credentials, impeccable references, the best people all over the globe. By then I was hoping for someone to perform sheer miracles, to reverse the damage that had already been done. Once again, I refused to listen to his dissenting opinion and pressed him forward.' She smiled wanly.

'And here I am. At first it was devastating. It had finally begun to dawn upon me what I was actually doing to myself. I was despondent. That was when Laura showed up at my door.'

'Laura Spilwell sought you out?'

'Exactly. She was absolutely charming and lovely. She never said it, but I understood that she had come to support me, to somehow try to make up for what she felt her husband had done to me. She didn't try to make excuses for him or offer silly homilies, she was just . . . there for me. And we became friends.'

'You must have found a way to spend a good deal of time together, then.'

'I was amazed to discover that we had much in common. Laura came from an excellent family. She had traveled a lot. She was very familiar with my beloved Tuscany, she knew of my favorite places in Spain and France. She was a very fashionable woman, we could talk about so much. I invited her to join me on a few trips as well. Somehow she healed me, Detective Garvey. My bitterness began to vanish, my joy for life began to return. I learned to ignore this strange husk I had acquired, and at the same time to laugh at those who could only pretend to ignore it.' She laughed, a soft enchanting laugh.

'Now I feel bad for them, because they cannot see what really matters.'

'Ms. Solana, people have said that you are a very remarkable woman. I now see they understated.'

'You're most gracious, Detective. Now tell me, has this young inquisitive woman caused you the trouble you feared she might?'

'I don't think so. I think I got to her before she could do any real damage.'

'Dane Spilwell is going to jail, is he not?'

'Yes. He was sentenced to life imprisonment at Falcon Island. There will be an appeal but I don't think it will do any good.'

'I still do not understand why he would kill Laura. It didn't make sense. I would have thought he was a smarter man than that, more perceptive.'

'Murder is seldom an intelligent action, Ms. Solana. But what exactly do you mean about him being more perceptive?'

'Well, for example, did he not realize

that Laura knew he was seeing another woman?'

'Maybe you should tell me more about this.'

'I was here in your city for the last few weeks she was alive. We got together several times to talk and do things together. She seemed lonely and very unhappy. She had learned that her husband was involved with another woman. I don't mean just a casual indiscretion or anything like that. She was convinced that he was very seriously involved with someone, and that he was going to press her for a divorce.'

'Did Laura ever tell you how she had come to that conclusion?'

'Well, wives, girlfriends, they always know, don't they?'

But not boyfriends, thought Jilly. Not Mark Zanello. Aloud she simply said, 'I have observed that's often the case, yes.'

'Little subtleties we pick up on, don't we? Especially if we are at all perceptive. Laura was a brilliantly perceptive woman. She was possessed of an exquisite sensitivity. She knew.'

'But Dane had not approached her about a divorce?'

'Oh no. He was undoubtedly concerned about appearances. And perhaps there was a problem with the woman as well. I would not be surprised if she were also married. But Laura was convinced everything was going to come to a crescendo, so to speak, before very long. And she was resigned to agree to a divorce as well. There would have been no contest on her part.'

'So you're saying Dane could have simply, er, eliminated Laura from his life in a much simpler and easier way? Forgive me if that sounds blunt.'

Surprisingly, Clea laughed, this time with gusto. 'I'm quite relieved, it would seem I don't have to walk as carefully around you as I thought I might! You put it quite succinctly, Detective. It's no laughing matter, of course, but yes, it all seemed quite senseless to me. Could Dane Spilwell have been that obtuse? Could he not have realized his deception was not perfect, that it had ... ' she reached for words ...

'holes like a leaky boat?'

'Laura was on to him,' Jilly nodded.

'Precisely. It was clear to her that her husband was infatuated with this other woman, whoever she was. She said there were times he acted like a schoolboy rather than a sophisticated world-famous surgeon.'

'Wow,' said Jilly. 'I have to admit, I had no idea about this.'

Clea's eyes widened. 'But you're the detective!' She smiled mischievously.

'We never needed to explore this side of things. Everything was cut and dried, it was as clear a case as we ever saw.'

'Would any of this information have made a difference to your case?' Clea asked with interest.

'No. Not really. But what does surprise me is that the defense never introduced any of this. Possibly it could have been incriminating, but a sharp attorney could have spun some of this as argument against his motive. The motive was the weakest part of the case. Well, it wasn't weak, just less strong. Basically, the prosecution argues motive, means, and opportunity. We had means and opportunity down cold.'

Clea nodded. 'The murder weapon. The fingerprints. The doctor's lack of an alibi. And so forth.'

'Right.'

Clea shrugged. 'For some reason, the defense refused to consider these things as having advantage. Or perhaps they did not know.'

'Didn't know?'

'Dane Spilwell was, what's the expression, playing his cards close to his chest? For whatever reason, he may have felt the time was not yet opportune to publicize his mystery lover, even to his lawyer? Perhaps her own husband did not know? Perhaps she just was not ready to commit to him as he was willing to commit to her? Maybe she wasn't ready to leave her own marriage as of yet?'

'Wow.' Jilly suddenly felt like a total naif. Here she was, someone considering herself to be a hardened and experienced detective, feeling out of her league from the woman with whom she sat. 'Wow'? Had she really just said

'Wow' not once but twice?

Clea smiled and waved a hand. 'But none of this is of real import now, is it? What's happened has happened.' The smile faded. 'It's a tragedy. An awful tragedy. A lovely, wonderful woman, full of life and kindness and generosity, was taken from us, and for totally senseless causes. I'm glad that justice will be done to her killer.'

There was a rushing sound as one of Clea's assistants operated the espresso machine.

'You must try the biscotti,' Clea smiled.

7

Kovetsky gestured with her thumb at the coffee shop. 'He's in there. I better not go in with you, he wouldn't want to be seen with me in public.' She glanced up and down at Dan.

'You don't look too cop right now. If you're cool he'll be okay.' She gave him a quick smile, which Dan returned. It was a cold wet morning and the both of them were hunkering down, Kovetsky in her uniform jacket and Dan in his windbreaker.

'Thanks,' he said.

'He'll be in his usual dark hoodie. You won't be able to miss him.'

'And you say his name is Hojo?'

'Yep. Been a help to me a few times now. I helped his sister out of a jam a while back. But it only goes so far.'

'Hojo? Really?'

'It's his real name. No kidding, Howard Johnson.'

'Are you serious?'

Kovetsky raised her hands and her eyebrows simultaneously. 'What can I tell ya, Detective Lee?'

'By the way, Dan is just fine,' Dan replied. 'Greatly appreciated.'

'Anytime, Dan. And you can call me Sandy.' She gave him an up-and-down look and a smirk and turned away.

Pearson's was a small old-school coffee shop, not overly full at the moment. It was in a neighborhood that was on the fringes of the Roland 29s territory but considered neutral territory by the local gangs.

Dan saw a young man in a dark hooded sweatshirt and knit cap, sitting alone at the long counter with a plate of eggs in front of him. He ordered a cup of coffee and sat himself down about two seats away. This had to be Hojo.

He was in his early teens, but already had the hardened and confident look of an older boy. He gave Dan little more than a cursory glance, continuing to simply sit and look straight ahead at nothing in particular, as if lost in scowling thought.

Dan's coffee came quickly. He took a sip and said quietly, 'So you must be Hojo.' Neither of them looked at the other.

'You the cop? Kovetsky told me you're cool,' the boy mumbled, so low he could hardly be heard.

'Got no interest in doing anything to you,' Dan said. He pulled out his phone and laid it on the counter, just to look as if he were doing something. 'Just trying to find out some info. You heard about the body on Pilsen yesterday?'

'Sure. Everybody heard about that.'

'They're saying it was a 29s killing.'

Hojo snorted. 'Who's sayin' that? That's crazy.'

'You're saying it's not?'

'Hell, no. No way. That boy, he wasn't no gangster. Not from our 'hood, not from nobody's. He was like a hipster, you know? Someone prob'ly killed him somewhere, brought him and stuffed him in that building to get him outa the way.'

Out of the mouths of babes, thought Dan.

'Not an initiation, like, some kid

earning his bones?'

Hojo shook his head, still looking straight ahead. 'That ain't how it's done. And I woulda heard about any, you know, membership drives. Haven't been no jumpin' in, these past coupla weeks.'

'No way a couple of the guys might have gotten into it with him and popped him?'

'Nobody in the 29s would roll that way. That's an insult.' Hojo glanced about a bit apprehensively. He clearly did not want to be caught here. 'And if anybody had been popped, proper like, you know, we'd know about it all over. That'd be the point, you know?'

'The hipsters don't come down there to buy?' Dan asked. 'They don't get robbed, or get disrespectful and in fights?'

'Oh yeah. Little rich boys out slummin'. Their money's green too. Once in a while they get taken. I don't mean hurt, I mean like what you call *robbed*. But nothing like this ever happened. Nothing like what you're talkin' about *did* happen.'

'You're positive?' Dan asked. He felt

like he should be talking dramatically out of the side of his mouth, like in an old detective movie. He kept looking down at his phone screen. 'Kovetsky said you'd be straight with me. I'm not looking to get you in trouble. I just need to know what might have gone down.'

'Wasn't no 29s,' Hojo repeated, scooping up a forkful of eggs and washing it down with a gulp of orange juice. 'Look, lemme explain something to you. Two caps in the head, right? Two. In the head. That's how he got it?'

'That's right.'

'Around here, that means something specific. Very specific. You understand? Serious reprimand. Something like that happen, it's a message, we all know about it soon enough. Not how you treat a white boy that turned the wrong street.'

'Got you,' Dan said.

'Somebody from outside the 'hood done this. Guaranteed. Take it to your bank next time you go.' He looked about furtively once again. 'Not comfortable talking much more here and now, okay?'

'Got it,' Dan said, gulping down his

cup and standing up. 'Appreciate the help.'

'You can grab my breakfast if you wanta be appreciative,' the boy said, still eating and looking straight ahead. Despite his youth, Dan could see he already looked hard and even haggard.

'No problem,' Dan said and picked up the boy's check as well as his own, walking to the cash register.

★ ★ ★

'So was he of any help?' Kovetsky said on the other end of the line.

'They sure grow up fast in the 29s, don't they? He's like, fifteen?' Dan was on a corner, in front of his car, concentrating to hear on his phone over the street noise.

'He's practically an elder statesman. We see nine, ten year olds on the corners all the time. A lot of them have gone cold and dead behind the eyes by their mid-teens. Hojo's still got a spark.'

'He says it's nothing the 29s would have done. Not their style. And you say I can believe him?'

'As far as it goes, yeah. I tend to agree. I've been thinking about that. Two bullets to the head, when I see that — and it's not all that often — it's usually a statement of policy. Hojo thinks it's a dump from outside the neighborhood, right?'

'Right.'

'I think you can believe him.'

'Would he have told me if it *was* something the 29s had done?'

'Can you tell me what he said specifically?'

Dan related the gist of the conversation.

'My read? If he knew of something and didn't want to get too involved, he would have approached it differently. Would have clammed up totally. The way he was telling you was as important as what he was saying, how I look at it.'

'Okay, Thanks again, Sandy.'

'Dan and Sandy it is, then,' she said. 'You need to come down here more often, Dan, get a better feel for this part of town. Totally job related, you understand.'

'I'll keep the invite in mind.'

Dan's phone buzzed. His Lieutenant, Hank Castillo.

'Detective Lee? You might want to get back here. We've got a present waiting for you and Garvey.'

'What do you mean, Lieutenant?'

'They got your Toyota. Picked up a guy driving around in it. The officers are bringing him over now. Better inform Garvey as well.'

'I'm on it.' He rang off and began to dial Jilly.

★ ★ ★

'Stokely James Richardson,' Jilly read off the rap sheet she held. 'A.k.a. Skeeter, a.k.a Skeets. Nothing really horrible on here, you know? This is kind of surprising to me, what we have going on here now.'

Stokely was a tall, thin and bony man possibly in his late thirties, with a scraggly soul patch on his chin and blond dreadlocks that looked as if they were last washed in the previous millennium.

He sat in a plain gray metal chair at a

plain gray metal table in the interview room, scratching himself and rocking back and forth slightly. He didn't seem to be focusing on anything very well at the moment.

Dan sat across from him. Jilly was still standing.

'So help us out here, would you, Stokely? How did you happen to be in that car that doesn't belong to you this morning?'

Stokely shrugged, staring more or less straight ahead. 'Found it. I was gonna return it.'

'Return it. How nice of you. You're just a regular citizen, Stokely. And I suppose you were going to return the phone as well?' She held up a plastic bag containing a smart phone.

'Man, I don't know nothin' about that.'

'And here it was on the seat right next to you. Funny thing, there are four calls on it that seem to have been made in the past few hours, and how much do you want to bet when we track those numbers down, they'll belong to people who know you? Want to take that bet?'

He shook his head vaguely. He didn't seem to be quite all there.

'The officers who pulled you over got you on possession as well. Possession of what appear to be marijuana and possibly crystal methamphetamine.'

'Man, those were, like, in the car, I had nothin' to do with any of that.'

'Hmm. Do tell. But here's what *really* makes me wonder, Stokely.' Jilly held up another plastic bag, this one containing a black wallet and a watch.

'These were under the seat, where you probably stowed them for safe keeping until you could *return* them, right?'

He looked up at the wallet with a start. Finally something seemed to register. 'Huh? I don't know nothin' about no wallet. I never saw that!'

Jilly let the bag dangle back and forth as she held the top with two fingers. 'So we're not going to find your fingerprints anywhere on this, right?'

'No, no way! I never even saw them, I sure as hell didn't touch them! What is that?'

'Well, it's a wallet, of course. And a

watch, see? They belonged to a man named Mark Zanello. You didn't happen to know him, did you?'

'Never heard of him! I don't know no Marks at all!'

'Mark showed up dead yesterday, Stokely.'

'What! I don't know nothin' about that!'

'So,' interjected Dan, 'how did you happen to be driving in his car? If you don't know him, you're not going to tell me a perfect stranger lent you his car and then went and got himself killed.'

'And,' Jilly added, 'you're going to tell us you know nothing about the blood in the trunk, which we think is going to turn out to be Mark Zanello's?'

Stokely shook his head as if to try to clear the obvious confusion. Jilly and Dan had no doubt he had been dipping into his bags of goodies before the officers had pulled him over.

'Okay, look, I boosted the car, okay? Yeah sure. It was just sitting there. Doors and windows open. Keys in the ignition! But I really was gonna return it, okay? I mean, I figured I'd just borrow it for a while. That's a lousy neighborhood, you know? Who knows, someone might'a broke into it or stolen stuff out of it?' His sad grin exposed multiple missing teeth and a few that hadn't seen dental care since long before his last shampoo. 'I was, you know, doin' the guy a favor, you wanta look at it like that!'

'And where,' sighed Dan patiently, 'did you find this car that you so gallantly rescued from the vandals and thieves?'

Stokely thought hard. It was work to which he was clearly unaccustomed. Dan thought he might soon smell his head burning.

'It was onna street, over around 33rd. Somewhere over there.'

Dan had an image of Stokely wandering down the street, furtively trying car doors as he walked, until he found one that was open.

'And you just happened to notice this one?'

'There was a ticket on the windshield, made me take a closer look.'

'When? When did you take it, I mean?'

'Aw, sometime yesterday, I guess. Just before dark.'

'And you've been driving it around ever since?'

'Naw, I parked it near my place last night, locked it up good, crashed out.'

'Looks like you made a little shopping trip this morning to fill your cart.'

Stokely shrugged.

So here's the thing we have to get back to, Stokely. The guy who owned the car, the phone, the wallet, all of which were in your possession. He's dead!'

'I got nothin' to do with that.' A light seemed to go on somewhere in his brain. He looked up suddenly and said, 'I think I'm gonna need a lawyer.'

'Magic words,' muttered Jilly, sweeping up the items she had brought into the room. 'We're done here, partner.'

'Too bad,' said Dan as he rose, picking up his own notes. 'We might have been able to help you out here, Stokely. Copping an attorney that sure makes us think you might be guilty of something really serious this time.'

Stokely shook his head, crossed his

arms. He looked frightened. 'I didn't do nothin' and I got nothin' more to say.'

'Okay, okay. I'm assuming you'll be wanting a public defender?' Norland Towers was not going to be available for this one. Jilly felt fairly confident about that.

★   ★   ★

They shut the door on Stokely awaiting his defender.

'33rd Street isn't all *that* far away from the building on Pilsen,' Dan observed. 'It's a bit of a walk, but conceivably Mark might have parked there and walked over.'

'You're thinking Stokely's tale is true?' Jilly asked.

'Maybe yes, maybe no. His jacket is all drug and burglary stuff, a stolen car or two. Nothing violent. No armed robbery, no assault, no possession of a firearm, no carjacking, nothing like that.'

'Doesn't mean he couldn't have done it, maybe if something went bad.'

'You're right. But I don't know. This guy is a burn brain.'

'Meth heads commit murders,' Jilly observed. 'Stupid ones too.'

'No gun,' Dan continued. 'Nothing in the car, anyway, nothing on him.'

'Even burn brains can think straight enough to dispose of a murder weapon. Wouldn't be the first time for either of us.'

'Yeah. But then there's this.' Dan leafed through the papers he had in his hand and held one out. 'The parking warrants on the car. Most of them are from the opposite side parking on street cleaning days around Mark's apartment. He apparently just ignored several of them.'

Jilly looked the list over and nodded.

'Then there's this one. Not gone to warrants yet. In fact it's only a few days old. Look at the address.'

'Vega near 33rd Street,' Jilly read.

'I think this doofus might just be telling us the truth.'

*   *   *

'So what've you got there?' Dan asked, eyeing the cardboard evidence box on

168

Jilly's desk. She had unsealed it and was extracting various items, laying them out in front of her.

'Got this from the evidence room. They hadn't sent it over to Records yet. Lucky break there. It's the Spilwell case.'

'Looking for the link,' Dan said.

'Yeah.' Jilly drew that word out like a long, resigned sigh. 'It's sure looking like there's something there.'

'But you're not convinced Spilwell is innocent?'

'I don't *want* *to* believe that, Dan. It was open and shut clear.'

'Cop heart versus cop brain,' Dan nodded. 'We have to follow the evidence.'

'Yeah. Pull up a chair, help me muddle through this.'

Jilly walked him through the steps of their investigation and the evidence. She started by describing the discovery of the body and the first conversation she and Reggie had with Dane Spilwell.

'He had a story about being in all night. But there was camera footage in the building's garage of him coming in and parking in his space around midnight. He couldn't adequately explain that.' She leafed through the loose-leaf binder that contained all her reports. 'Laura was stabbed by a carving knife, a fairly ordinary one that you found shoved down the storm drain not far away. It turned out to be part of a set of knives in the Spilwell kitchen. They were in a butcher-block case and the one was conspicuously missing. He had no explanation of why it was missing, said it had been misplaced for several days. It was easy enough to match the murder weapon specifically to the set. And of course it had a print of his on it.'

'Was it ever explained how Laura ended up in that alley?' Dan asked. 'She was expected at her book club, right? That was a couple of miles away in another part of town.'

'We never found her phone but got her phone records,' Jilly said, leafing through to the relevant page. 'The last call she received was at eight twenty-five P.M. The number turned out to be a public phone.'

'Public phone? There's still such a thing?'

'Yeah. Pay phone at a convenience store.

A Ready-Rite on Webley. No working security cameras anywhere around.'

'She made a call out after that, right?'

'Yes, to the St. Ashby residence. She told her friend she'd be late for the book club, she had to make another stop.'

'You figured Spilwell hadn't come home, he called her from there and lured her somewhere. Convinced her to take a detour, maybe to meet him at that restaurant she liked, Monica's.'

'Exactly. It all fit together. The Ready-Rite was pretty much directly between Spilwell's office and the alleyway. It would have been an easy and efficient route. He would have known she would park in that lot, maybe even told her to park there. And he laid in wait.'

'And then set it up so it would look like a robbery-mugging gone bad. That's all plausible. But the knife, that seems all wrong. If he went to that much trouble to make it look anonymous, why use a weapon that was so identifiable?'

'We went over that. Best explanation, it was what he could find. Maybe despite the apparent careful planning, he had thrown it all together at the last minute. There were certain indications of that. Anyway, we figured he thought he could toss the knife far enough down the drain that it wouldn't be found. Maybe he hoped for it to be washed away.' Jilly shrugged. 'It was perhaps the most tenuous part of our case, but for us it fit. We were afraid Towers would hit it hard, but somehow he didn't.'

'That,' Dan nodded, 'and the motive angle was weak.'

'When the evidence is that solid,' Jilly replied, 'you can work around the motive.'

'And again, Towers didn't hit that as hard as he could, did he?'

'No. He did bring it up but, in retrospect, he could have hammered at us with it. He pulled his punches. Not very noticeably, but still . . . '

'Sure seems pretty solid,' Dan mused. 'Open and shut.'

'But something about this case seems to be riling up somebody. What exactly, and why, I haven't got a clue.' Jilly peered at the sheets in the binder in front of her.

'I need to go over this stuff one more time.'

'We,' said Dan, holding out a hand. 'We're a 'we,' partner. Fresh pair of eyes. Can't hurt. Hand me over something.'

8

The offices of the prestigious firm of Towers and Bridges were located on the top floor of a tall downtown building. As they rode the wood-paneled elevator up, Dan remarked to Jilly, 'Appropriate, don't you think: Towers and Bridges, way up here in the sky?'

'Norland Towers and Harrington Bridges. Couple of prep school Ivy Leaguers. Reggie used to make a joke that nobody working here was allowed to have an actual first name.'

Norland Towers was not one of her favorite people, nor was he looked upon with much favor by any of her colleagues. He was celebrated in some quarters for his uncanny success at acquittals in high profile trials, generally on behalf of clients who could afford his spectacular charges or who promised a further measure of celebrity.

Jilly was a firm believer in the judicial

principle of presumption of innocence, but when she was the one who had done the hard work of gathering and analyzing the evidence and evolving an understanding of what it all indicated, it was difficult to see some of Towers' victories as anything but a triumph of manipulation over the truth.

Towers himself was smug and arrogant, not a man she would have liked even if he happened to be on her side in the courtroom. She had never really gotten to know him, nor did she really want to.

On the phone Jilly had been told that Towers would be in court today but that they would be able to speak with his assistant, Cynthia Grymes. She only kept them waiting around ten minutes. Dan remarked it was the most sumptuous waiting area in which they had ever had to cool their heels.

She finally arrived and ushered them back to a conference room, where they sat in dark leather chairs around a table of polished dark wood.

Grymes herself was buttoned-up, serious and self-possessed, and Jilly had the feeling that if she ever smiled, her face might actually crack. She sat straight up, now and then adjusting her stylish glasses but otherwise remaining almost stock still.

She asked how she might be of assistance to them.

'It's our understanding that several days ago a young woman named Kerry Moran came to these offices to present to Mr. Towers evidence she felt might indicate Dane Spilwell's innocence.'

'Oh yes. I remember. Last Friday. I was the one who spoke to her. Mr. Towers was out of town. She had a flash drive that she asked me to give to Mr. Towers. You know, a plug-in storage device for a computer?'

'Yes, we're familiar with them. And she explained why she felt the information was relevant to the case?'

'Yes, somewhat. Some kind of a story about a photograph and having encoun-tered the person in the picture on the night of the murder. She was scattered. But she was clearly very earnest in believing the photograph would be exculpatory.'

'And you didn't think so, Ms. Grymes?'

'Well, I have to say, she wasn't very compelling to my mind. She was passionate, but she did not persuade. But it wasn't my call, after all. I told her I would make sure that Mr. Towers got the flash drive, and asked for her contact information — which she told me was also on the flash drive, the whole story.'

'And you passed it on to Mr. Towers and told him what she had said?'

'Oh, of course.'

'When was that?'

'When he returned to the office, Monday morning.'

'Is there any chance he might have seen the photograph or the files on the drive before then?' Dan interjected.

'Doubtful, since he was out of town. He told me he returned to the city late Sunday night. But it was left to his attention along with other matters before I left Friday night. Had he returned early, he certainly could have seen it. But I spoke with him first thing in the morning on Monday, to fill him in on office affairs, and it seemed obvious that was the first he had heard of it.'

'And when you told him about it, what was his reaction?'

'He said he'd look into it. Perhaps an hour later he called me in and told me that Ms. Moran's photograph was inconclusive. There was no way to be sure the person in the picture was Dane Spilwell, and the enhancements that had been applied actually made it appear to be an attempt to alter an image. He said that even if it could be argued that it was Dane Spilwell in the photograph, it could conceivably do more harm than good for many reasons. It suggested that he was having an extramarital affair at the time his wife was murdered, which would only add motive, while doing absolutely nothing to establish a credible alibi. He said the ongoing appeal could be seriously jeopardized if the photograph came to light and I should ignore it.'

'Did he tell you to contact Kerry Moran and tell her that?'

'No, he said that from what I had told him about her, she seemed to be a bit of a 'loose cannon,' that was the precise term

178

he used. He said we should ignore her, have nothing to do with her, and that I should inform our receptionists to not let her speak to anyone if she should return.'

'That's rather curious, don't you think?' Jilly asked.

Grymes adjusted her glasses while staring at Jilly, never changing her glacial lack of expression.

'Not really. This office gets its share of . . . shall we call them *unhelpful* individuals? Many of them are quite well intentioned but, well, a bit divorced from reality. We've learned that any kind of attention is taken as encouragement of a sort, that we're better off ignoring them.'

'Until they go away,' said Dan.

Grymes leveled her iceberg stare at him. 'Yes, Detective. We're extremely busy here and don't need irrelevant distractions.'

'I'm sure you are,' Jilly smiled. 'Busy, that is. Do you still have the flash drive that Kerry Moran gave you?'

'No, Mr. Towers had it and said he was going to securely dispose of it. He didn't want the slightest possibility of it falling into anyone else's hands.'

'Do you know if Mr. Towers would have discussed this matter with anyone else in the office? Would he have considered, perhaps, that this was a situation that needed to be further addressed?'

'Not to my knowledge. I'm his administrative aide and just about everything goes through me. He did not ask me to pursue it with anybody.'

'And he didn't seem concerned that she might have taken her photograph and story elsewhere, to other people?'

'He didn't seem at all concerned about that, no. He dismissed her as a crank.'

'And has he ever brought the subject up again since?'

'No, never. Clearly we consider it a dead matter.' Grymes actually made an almost imperceptible twitch, as if she were growing impatient.

Jilly and Dan glanced at each other. This one had run its course. They both rose from the table.

'Thank you for your help, Ms. Grymes, we appreciate it.'

Cynthia Grymes led them down a carpeted corridor toward the reception area. There were nicely-framed photographs and graphics along the walls. As they walked, she looked back at Jilly. 'If I might ask what importance this all might have?'

'Just a routine inquiry,' Jilly smiled back. She paused at a photograph. 'This is Mr. Towers, isn't it?'

Grymes stopped and looked at the picture. 'Yes, that was last year at the Legal Society, when he received their Outstanding Professionalism Award.'

'That's his wife next to him on the dais then?'

'Yes, that's Mavis Towers.'

'I don't believe I've ever seen her before, in person or even a photograph.'

'Mrs. Towers does tend to avoid the limelight. She's a very private person, very seldom photographed.'

Jilly continued to stare. Dan stepped over and looked as well.

'She's quite lovely.'

'Yes, Mrs. Towers is stunningly beautiful, isn't she?'

'Is her hair really that color in real life? She was most fortunate to be born with such a beautiful hair color. We're both redheads but I can hardly say my hair color is anything like hers.'

'If anything, in person it's even more striking.' Grymes was clearly uncomfortable with small talk and wanted them to move on and leave her to her agenda, but Jilly persisted.

'And it goes so well with that shade of green of her dress. I bet she wears that color quite a bit. And those emeralds. Is she partial to emeralds?'

'I really couldn't tell you,' Grymes smiled almost painfully. 'I'm sorry, but I really have pressing matters, if there's nothing else . . . ?'

'Of course.' Jilly kept smiling as she turned away from the photo on the wall. 'We can find our way out, please don't let us keep you. And thank you for your help.'

They were in the elevator before either of them said another word. Jilly muttered, 'That SOB. It's her! It's his wife. And he knew.' Then she fell silent again until they were in the car and Dan was pulling away from the curb.

Dan could hear Jilly cussing under her breath as he drove. 'He beats us all the time,' she said. 'But this time he didn't. He didn't *want* to. His old friend, Dane Spilwell. He scuttled the case, left him out to dry. He must have. He'll blow the appeal as well.'

'That's something that would take a lot of finesse,' Dan observed. 'And it's a pretty outrageous idea, you have to admit.'

Jilly sat thoughtfully for a long moment. 'Now that I've got the idea in my head, I can kind of see it, Dan. Subtle things. Certain things he didn't push as hard as he could have. Certain things he let drop. The man's a master in the courtroom.'

'So you're thinking, Spilwell was fooling around with Towers' wife, Towers knew, but Spilwell did *not* know he knew? So Towers got back at him by sabotaging his defense?'

'Pretty wild, huh? Yeah. That is exactly what I am thinking.'

'Let's suppose for a moment you're right. It's a stretch, I'm not sure I can get my own head around this one, but let's just suppose. What does this mean, that Spilwell is really innocent?'

Jilly sighed. 'I don't know. Not necessarily. It could be argued he wanted her out of the way. But then, Clea told me Laura would have given him the divorce. I just don't know.'

'Is there some way this could relate to Mark Zanello? I mean, let's suppose Spilwell is being railroaded by his attorney, whether he's guilty or not. Suddenly Kerry's photo shows up, and her story about her and Mark in the restaurant. This could throw a huge monkey wrench into the works, couldn't it?'

'Someone threatens Kerry — or at least attempts to shut her up. Mark gets eliminated. Wait a minute.' She dug into her bag for her notebook and flipped through it. 'There's one other witness that she mentioned, and what happened to him? The restaurant. *A Light in the Tower*. The waiter. She called him Satch.'

She grabbed her phone. A couple of calls later she had reached the manager of *A Light in the Tower* and was asking about a waiter who worked there named Satch.

'You must mean Mort Blessing. Everybody calls him Satch.'

'Mort? Really? I understand he recently quit, is that right?'

'Yes, rather suddenly in fact. He's a musician and he got some kind of sudden offer in someplace like Chicago, I think he said.'

'He just up and quit, no notice?'

'He felt really bad about it. He's worked here for a while and we all like him. He's one of our most popular servers. But he said the offer came out of the blue, it was an enormous opportunity to play with some major band and he couldn't afford to turn it down. They needed him to leave that night. So I wished him well and reluctantly let him go. Well, maybe it wasn't all that willingly, but what could I do? I mean, after all, he's a musician first and a waiter second, isn't that always the case?'

'And you don't remember who the offer was from or any other details?'

'I'm sorry, no. Honestly, I was more focused on the fact I was losing a waiter I needed badly. But he was incredibly excited. He said he couldn't believe his luck. This was a once in a lifetime chance.'

'Did he leave a forwarding address, someplace to send his last paycheck, anything like that?'

'No, I agreed to settle up his paycheck right then. We've got a good history. And he said he'd contact me when he had a regular address there. Chicago, I'm pretty sure.'

'What day was that?'

'Let's see. It was Sunday. He was leaving on a red-eye flight.'

Jilly thanked the manager and hung up, dropping the phone back into her bag.

'By another strange coincidence, the other witness has left town. Chicago, the manager thinks. An unbelievable job offer.'

Dan shook his head. 'I'm not a fan of coincidence. This sounds really hinky.'

186

''Hinky'?' said Jilly. 'Did you really just say that? Are you trying to talk like cops on TV now, Dan? 'Hinky'? Really? Have you ever actually heard anybody say that?'

She laughed in spite of herself.

Dan shrugged. 'Just seemed appropriate. Okay, note to self. Avoid 'hinky' from here on out.'

'Anyway, for the record I agree with you, this is not coincidence. And now I'm wondering if Kerry might really be in some kind of possible danger.'

The tones of Stravinsky cried out. She looked at the caller name on her screen. Speak of the devil.

'Yes, Kerry, what's up?'

'Detective Garvey, I just got another call from Laura's brother. He said it's urgent I meet him right away.'

'What did he say exactly?'

'Just that it was vitally important and how soon could I meet him in the same park where he met me last time. He sounded really anxious.'

'What did you tell him?'

'I said I had to clear a couple things — that's a laugh — and that I'd call him

187

right back. Then I called you. Thank God I got through.'

'All right, listen, Kerry. We're coming by to get you. Do not — do not under any circumstance — go to meet him alone. Do you understand? How far away from the park are you?'

'Oh, five or ten minutes, it's close.'

'All right, call him back. Tell him you can meet him in — ' she glanced at her watch and did quick calculations. 'Tell him a half hour. No, forty minutes. Tell him whatever you need to. Make it clear you're serious about meeting him but there's no way you can be there for forty minutes. Got it?'

'Sure.'

'And call me back afterwards to let me know if he agreed or not. Got that?'

'Got it.' She rang off. Jilly turned to Dan, already dialing her phone again.

'Something's up. The 'brother' got back in contact, wants to see her right away.' She put a call into Lieutenant Castillo. When his aide answered she rapidly laid out the situation. She waited while Castillo himself came on, described the situation in greater detail, and requested a backup unit. She said they were now en route to meet Kerry Moran, and stressed that having a low profile might be crucial, so as not to scare away the person meeting with her.

Dan accelerated the car through traffic towards Kerry's apartment. 'You're thinking she really could be in danger,' he said.

'A guy deliberately misrepresenting himself in order to meet with her, and I'm starting to think he's the same guy who called to scare her later that night, now for some reason he's decided he needs to come back and try something else. We can't take a chance.'

Kerry called back shortly to say that 'Ryan' had agreed to meet her in forty-five minutes at the same bench where they had met before.

'Okay, Kerry. We'll be in front of your apartment house in about ten minutes. Don't come out to wait for us, just in case anybody is looking for you. We've got an unmarked car, I'll call you on your phone when we're here. Just wait for us in the lobby, stay out of sight from the street. Okay?'

★   ★   ★

Sunset Park was its formal name but most people in the city simply referred to it as the Park. It was a green area covering about four city blocks, with one entrance road on each of two sides. Two uniformed officers had showed up to join them. Jilly directed them to enter from the far side and approach the bench where Kerry had agreed to meet her caller, but to stay back out of sight. She and Dan would do the same thing from this side.

It was three minutes to the agreed meeting time and Jilly told Kerry to start walking in.

'We'll be a little behind you. You hopefully won't be able to see us, but we'll never let you out of our sight,' she told Kerry, who was beginning to look quite apprehensive.

'Do you think I'm in some danger here?' Kerry asked. 'Should I be worried?'

'No, I don't think so,' Kerry replied,

hoping she sounded more sure of that than she actually felt. 'You said he didn't seem threatening. And there are people all around right now, it's very public. But we need to talk to him. We don't want to scare him away. So we'll let you approach him first. Then we'll take over. You ready?'

Kerry nodded but she looked less than confident.

'It's going to be okay, Kerry. Go on now.'

Kerry turned and strode down the paved pathway that led over a small rise to a set of benches. It was chilly and overcast, and that had discouraged too many people from coming here, but there were still people scattered about: children and dogs playing, a couple of people sitting on benches reading.

Dan moved off across the grass to position himself on another side of the bench that Kerry had described as her rendezvous point.

Jilly stopped at the top of the short rise and watched. There was a man sitting on a far bench, arms crossed, moving his head back and forth. He looked, from this distance at least, to be perhaps in his fifties. He saw Kerry approaching and waved.

Jilly pulled out a walkie-talkie and thumbed the button to talk to Dan and the uniforms. 'That looks like him. She's approaching the bench now. Everybody hold steady.'

The man rose to greet her, they shook hands, and they sat down. He began to speak animatedly to her. Jilly couldn't hear what was being said but it was clearly being said with a sense of urgency.

'All right, let's close in, slowly. Don't spook him.'

Jilly had taken about four steps toward them when the man's head shot up. He looked around and saw Dan coming down the grassy hill from the other direction. He bolted out of the seat and grabbed Kerry's arm, yelling something at her. She wrenched her arm back in alarm and recoiled from him. He looked around and saw Jilly also coming. He sprinted off at an angle away from them both. Jilly hollered and then yelled into the walkie-talkie, 'He's moving!'

Dan instantly changed his course and broke into a run across the grass at a path to intercept him. The man turned away, angling in towards Jilly, who was also now running. She had un-holstered her sidearm and had it in her hand as she moved.

'Police!' she shouted. 'Stop!'

The man saw the gun in her hand and froze. He skidded to a halt in the grass, struggling to keep his balance, and threw his hands up. It was almost comical.

Dan reached him first. The uniforms suddenly appeared as well. In another few moments, the four police officers had surrounded the man.

He was unarmed and suddenly indignant.

'What's going on here?' he demanded. 'Why are you chasing me? What's with the *guns*?'

'We just wanted to talk with you,' Dan said officiously, 'but you suddenly ran from us. That tends to make us suspicious.'

'How was I supposed to know you were the police?' he sputtered. 'For all I knew, you were someone meaning me and the young lady some harm!'

'You were expecting someone like that?' Jilly asked.

'As a matter of fact, possibly, yes!'

'All right, let's go talk about this, any objection?'

'Am I under arrest?'

'Not yet,' said Dan.

'We're asking you to come voluntarily with us,' Jilly said.

He looked back and forth at them, and at Kerry, who was now carefully approaching the gathering.

'All right,' he said.

★ ★ ★

The station interview rooms tended to the sterile side: functional but not overly comfortable, painted in muted beiges and greys, with hard backed chairs and simple heavy tables. They had sent Kerry home with the uniforms and driven the man back with them.

He had voluntarily shown them identification, a state Private Investigator's license in the name Earl Ryan and a driver's license with the same name. Now he sat across the table from them, all three of them holding Styrofoam cups of rather dreadful coffee.

'I wasn't trying to threaten the girl,' he was insisting. 'I was trying to help her.'

'You told her your name was Ryan Hart. You said you were the brother of Laura Spilwell.'

He nodded. 'Yes. Yes, I did that.'

'You also approached her earlier,' Dan added. 'Told her the same thing. You deliberately misrepresented your identity to her. Want to tell us why?'

'I had a feeling she was wary of strangers. I needed to get her to meet me, so I could warn her.'

'Warn her of what, exactly?'

'I thought that what she was doing was going to get her in trouble.'

'What do you mean?' Jilly asked. 'What was she doing?'

'She was opening up a can of worms she knew nothing about.' He stared at them, arms crossed.

'How did you find out about her and

all this?' Dan asked. 'Maybe we should start at the beginning?'

Ryan shrugged. 'I was contacted by an attorney that I do occasional work for. He asked me to look into her.'

'And this attorney was . . . ?'

He hesitated.

'If this is all on the level, surely you can tell us who it was?'

'There's a possible issue of client privilege here,' he said, thinking it over.

'And there's a possible issue of us arresting you on various charges of endangering Miss Moran,' said Jilly pointedly.

Ryan nodded and pursed his lips. 'Norland Towers.'

'When did he contact you and what did he say?'

'He called me Saturday and asked me to check her out.'

'Saturday. You're sure of that?'

'Positive. Saturday morning. He said he wanted to meet me at my office. He seemed quite urgent for me to look into it. He said she was endangering one of his cases with irresponsible assertions, and that I needed to find out who she had been talking with and try to dissuade her from continuing. We spent a while talking and I got all the information.'

'So you contacted Kerry Moran after that?'

'The next day. I decided my wisest move was to approach her as 'Ryan Hart.' The impression I got was that she was a bit of a space cadet and could easily be spooked. That's what Mr. Towers was also concerned about. He stressed we needed to be diplomatic, to finesse her.'

'So your idea was to pretend to be a relative of the deceased.'

'Yeah. I called her up and asked her to meet me, put on a grieving sibling act.'

'How did you get her phone number?'

'She apparently gave her contact information to Mr. Towers in whatever she left for him. It was easy to reach her.'

'So you met with her, told her the family was concerned about dredging up whatever she had found, asked her to stop?'

'I practically begged her to stop. It was an Academy Award performance. I'm pretty good at that kind of play-acting.' He actually smiled heartily.

'And she told you, what, that she wouldn't try to talk to anyone else about her theories?'

'Well, no.' The smile faded. 'She said she'd have to think about it. I could kind of tell she wasn't going to cooperate. I reiterated that she was potentially causing more harm than good to the entire family, that I was speaking for all of them. I laid it on heavy, the guilt trip. She seemed like she'd be most receptive to that.'

'You apparently weren't aware that Laura Spilwell had no brother, in fact almost no family to speak of.'

Ryan shrugged. 'Didn't matter. I didn't figure she was the sharpest tool in the shed, if you know what I mean. All I needed was to get her to back off. I just made it up on the fly.'

'But that didn't seem to work. By any chance did you try to contact her again right after that?'

A deep sigh. Ryan looked down at his folded arms. 'Uh, yes. Yes, I did. I called her back Tuesday evening under another persona and tried a different approach.'

'What you mean is, you called her in the middle of the night and anonymously threatened her.'

'I said nothing that could be legally construed as threatening,' he said sharply. 'I didn't identify myself, but all I said was that she was intruding into areas that she didn't understand and she should stay out. It was not a threat, it was a warning.'

Jilly and Dan just stared at him. It was so quiet that they could hear the click of the minute hand on the old-fashioned wall clock.

'Maybe not the smartest way to play it, agreed,' Ryan finally admitted. 'But I was right in trying to head her off. What happened after that proves me out. That's why I went back again.'

'What do you mean?'

'Mr. Towers had a point. Somebody found out about what she was doing and may have had their own methods of dealing with it. I heard about her boyfriend being found in the old building.'

'How did you know about the connection?'

'The gal put *everything* in the stuff she left for him! Her whole story. She named the names and the places and the times. It was a damned book, rambling on and on! He had me review it. I remembered the name, Mark Zanello. Then the news came out about his body being found. I figured it *had* to have something to do with this. She's a nut but she's a sweet kid. I had to get in touch with her and talk her out of pursuing this any further. That was all I was trying to do, meeting up with her today. I swear it.'

'After your first two contacts with Kerry, did you contact Towers to tell him about your activity and her reaction?'

'I told him about the brother act. Not about the night call. In hindsight I decided that might be embarrassing. He seemed okay with my meeting with her and her reaction. He said okay, we'd just wait and see what would happen and I was done for now.'

'So you didn't happen to try to contact

any of the other people she named?' Dan asked.

'No, all he asked me to do was to talk to her. I guess he had a point, what she was doing really was dangerous.'

'Your two calls on Sunday and Tuesday came from different phones,' Jilly said.

'Yeah. I have several prepaid burners. Just buy 'em, put minutes on 'em. Pretty anonymous. They come in handy.'

'Yeah, I bet they do,' Jilly muttered.

'Hey, I haven't done anything wrong! I resent the implications! I'm on the up and up, and my clients are legitimate! I was just trying to help the girl! And my client as well!'

*   *   *

The remainder of the interview was fruitless. They left him in the interview room and headed down the hallway.

'Think we can hold him on anything?' Dan asked.

'We could come up with something. But why?'

'So you buy his story?'

'The only part that makes me wonder is that Towers would employ a guy that thick.'

'Think he'll call Towers when we let him go?'

Jilly shook her head. 'I'm hoping he's scared to talk to him now, that Towers will be angry at him for screwing up.'

'So Towers was back in town by Saturday, despite what he told his aide.'

'If he ever left at all.' Jilly stared at Dan. 'Sounds kind of *hinky*, doesn't it, partner?'

Dan winced good-naturedly. 'Indeed it does. So I guess that's going to be our word after all, huh?'

'In any case, I think Mr. Towers bears further scrutiny, wouldn't you say?'

★ ★ ★

Back into the squad room, Dan noted that he had new messages on his computer. He sat down and tapped them up.

'Got the records from Mark Zanello's phone,' he said, scrolling through a list.

Jilly peered at the screen over his shoulder.

After a short time he asked, 'He was killed Friday night, right? Around eight?'

'More or less.'

'He made no calls out for two or three hours before that. But . . . he received a call around seven fifteen.' Dan moved the computer's cursor over the number. 'Doesn't match any other incoming calls listed here.'

He opened a new window and tapped in instructions. Quickly he was into the department's reverse directory that listed according to telephone number.

'A pay phone. Do you believe it!' Dan said. '2435 Webley. Weren't we just talking about that street a while ago?'

'Yeah. The Ready-Rite where the last call was made to Laura Spilwell.'

'Just for the hell of it . . . ' Dan said, opening another browser window and typing further. 'The Ready-Rite is at 2435.' He turned and looked over his shoulder at an amazed Jilly. 'Our victim's last phone call came from the same place as Laura Spilwell's last call.'

Jilly's brain went into overdrive. There was no longer any way to deny a connection between the murders.

Dan perused the web page for the store number of the Ready-Rite, then picked up his phone and dialed. He spoke briefly, ending with, 'hold on to it. We'll be right over,' and hung up. Jilly was still silent, lost in thought.

'We might have caught a break,' Dan said. 'Something new has happened since the Spilwell case.'

'What do you mean, Dan?'

'I mean that there's now a security camera outside the Ready-Rite. A *working* one.' He rose from his desk. 'The manager's pulling last Friday's footage for us.'

⋆　⋆　⋆

'I've only been the manager here for a few weeks now, and one of my first priorities was to install a working security camera system.' The manager's name was Arjuna Patel and it was clear that his store's ambience was quite different from the way Jilly remembered it from a year ago. It was better illuminated, cleaner, more orderly, and the two people behind the counter looked as if they actually were concerned about doing their jobs rather than just waiting for their shifts to end. Patel was pointing with obvious pride to the security camera poised in a dark alcove over the doorway. They were standing just outside the store. The public telephone was several steps away, on a metal pedestal, weather-beaten plastic surrounding it top and sides. 'There have been several incidents in this store over the past months. Even a shooting. The previous management cared nothing for making it safer or more efficient. I set up several cameras inside and out. I want to upgrade this store, bring customers back. Perhaps even save a few jobs, including my own.'

Jilly was examining the camera. 'Someone using the phone over there might not even notice that camera's up there. It's silent and it's in a dark spot.'

'It's got a clear shot of the phone too,'

Dan noted. 'Many people use that phone?'

Patel shook his head. 'Not really. I'm surprised the company hasn't asked to have it removed. Or that the phone company hasn't done so on its own. This neighborhood tends to be overlooked in general.' He shrugged resignedly.

'So you have the tapes from last week?'

'Not tapes, everything is on digital file. You're lucky you called when you did. I keep the video files for about two weeks and if there is nothing noteworthy, I erase them.'

'So if we could see the videos from last Friday?' Jilly asked.

'Of course,' Patel said with a smile, motioning them inside. He had a small office in the back — really not much more than a storeroom with a cluttered desk. He picked up a computer disc in a paper sleeve and handed it to them.

'This is everything from Friday evening, from about noon to midnight. Everything is time coded as well.'

'Could we just give it a quick look on your equipment?'

'Certainly,' Patel said, walking to a DVD player and monitor on the wall. The monitor was currently showing a montage of images from his four security cameras in real time. He popped the disc into a slot and the image changed.

'Can we jump ahead to . . . ' Jilly turned to Dan. 'What time was the call?'

'Seven thirteen in the evening. Maybe we could start just a couple minutes ahead of that?'

Patel picked up a remote, pressing a button. The image fast-forwarded and the time signature in the upper right corner sped more rapidly. He stopped the forward motion at 19:11 and stepped back. Dan and Jilly moved in closer. The digital image showed the parking lot off the street directly in front of the entrance. The pay phone was on the far right. A few people walked in and out of the store. The front bumper of a car appeared as it pulled into a parking spot. Another bumper receded from the picture as the car backed out of its spot.

'The times don't agree,' Jilly said impatiently. The time signature had just changed to 19:14.

'There!' Dan said, pointing. 'There's our guy.'

A figure, a man, had entered the picture from the far right and was looking back and forth as he picked up the receiver on the phone. Possibly because he did not want to call attention to himself, he was not acting furtively or going to any effort to hide himself. Even in the relatively low resolution of the camera footage, his face was clear for several seconds as he spoke into the receiver and then hung it up.

'Oh my God,' Jilly muttered. She swallowed hard.

'Is that who I think it is?' Dan asked.

Jilly nodded. 'Yes. Yes, it is.'

★   ★   ★

'There's no way this could be a coincidence,' Dan said as he drove.

'I'm afraid not,' said Jilly, still stewing in her thoughts. 'We have to handle this carefully. We're only going to get one shot. We could blow this.'

'Agreed.'

'What we've got going for us is that he's been so sure things would go his way. He expected the body to remain undiscovered for a much longer time. He either figured there was still no security camera at the Ready-Rite or that the footage would be recorded over even if we could get that far. He's been wrong on a number of things but he thinks he's smart enough that things haven't gone *too* wrong.'

'As someone once told me,' Dan said, 'they think we're not that bright, but that they are. And almost always, they're not.'

'Smart person who said that,' Jilly said wryly. She had her phone out and called Kerry. Kerry answered after several rings and sounded terrible. Apparently the shock of everything had finally hit her.

'How are you holding up?'

'Not great, Detective. Today really scared me. I've really screwed up.'

'I'm sorry to bother you but I have a question, it might be important.'

'Shoot. Nobody here but me, I've got nothing but time.'

'You left a flash drive for Norland Towers, right?'

'Yes, one of those thumb-drive thingies.'

'Can you tell me exactly what was on that drive?'

She spoke slowly. 'I put together a little presentation, in a PDF format. Kind of like things we did at the magazine now and then. There was a high and low resolution copy of my enhanced photo, and an accompanying text describing the circumstances in detail and why I felt they were important. I had a feeling I might not get to talk to Mr. Towers myself and explain things so I wanted it all laid out for him.'

'And Ms. Grymes did not look at anything?'

'No, she just took it and said when Mr. Towers got back, she would make sure he saw it.'

'In that text, did you mention any of the other people at the restaurant that night? Mark or your friend the waiter, Satch?'

'Yes, I described the whole situation

carefully. I knew this could be valuable exculpatory evidence.' She had some trouble articulating those last two words. 'Well . . . I *thought* it was going to be. I guess it wasn't.'

'Kerry, was there contact information for you or anybody else in that text?'

'Uh-huh. My phone number and email address. I put Mark's phone number on there and the number to reach Satch at the restaurant.' Kerry paused for a long moment. 'You're saying that Mark's death *was* connected to what I did? Did I get him *killed*?'

'Take it easy, Kerry. No, I'm not saying anything like that. We're just looking into the threats you reported to us and I'm getting some further information. What I think you should do is get some rest. I'll talk to you in the next couple of days and maybe I'll have some news for you. In the meantime, just stay low and take care of yourself.' She considered the way Kerry's voice sounded, a little slurred. 'Umm . . . have you eaten tonight?'

'Crackers,' Kerry slurred. 'And some cheese.'

'Sounds like you've been washing it down with something too. Maybe you better go easy, okay?'

'Just trying to get through this,' Kerry said softly. Jilly could hear she was starting to cry. She attempted a few more supportive statements and then rang off. There was nothing more she could do. Kerry was in a downward spiral for the moment.

'Want to hear how I think we should handle this?' asked Dan as he took a corner.

'Go for it,' said Jilly.

'If Spilwell is protecting Mavis, he thinks the affair is still a secret . . . maybe if he decided that his silence was actually putting her in danger . . . '

'If he opens up, it might change everything.'

'I think it's worth a shot. We have to play a couple of the players. And if our scenario is right, we'll need to fill in a lot of the blanks. So here's what I propose . . . '

Jilly listened in wonder. It was close to what she had been considering, but, she had to admit, with some improvements. Her new partner might just work out.

'We've got a lot to do over this weekend,' she said. 'I'll push Castillo for some overtime. Let's hope it pans out.'

9

Saturday morning, Jilly made the drive to the Island.

Falcon Island would sound like a lovely place to anyone unaware that it was the site of one of the state's maximum security prisons. There was little else on the small island, in fact, but rocky tree-lined cliffs that were home to the isle's namesake bird. Anyone clever enough to escape the prison itself would have to contend with descending to the coast and dealing with the ferocious rip tides to try to get to the mainland. It was a facility that had seen few breakouts in its history.

This was the new home of Dr. Dane Spilwell.

'Well, Detective,' Spilwell said as he was led by a guard into the sparse meeting room. 'I'd like to tell you it's a pleasure to see you again, but you'll understand if I don't.' He did not smile.

He looked haggard and much older than he had in court.

The guard sat him down across the table from Jilly and stepped back. He silently glared at her.

'Totally understood, Doctor,' said Jilly, reaching into the briefcase she had already laid on the table. She held up a large blowup of a photograph and showed it to him. 'Is this you in this photo?'

Spilwell looked at it impassively and said nothing.

'Certainly looks like you. Do you by any chance remember the occasion on which this was taken?'

He said nothing, just looked at the picture.

'Suppose I were to tell you this was taken the night that your wife died?'

Still nothing in reply. Spilwell could have been a statue of a seated man in an orange jumpsuit.

'I assume you recognize the woman in the photo with you, her back to the camera? I think you know who she is. I'm told she's got beautiful flaming red hair in real life, and she's very partial to emeralds. Real ones, no doubt. A very classy woman, isn't she?'

Spilwell turned his eyes to glare at Jilly once again.

'Have you spoken to your attorney recently, Doctor?'

'Every day,' he said slowly.

'The person who gave me this? They took this picture last year. They brought it to your attorney, Norland Towers, last week. They thought it might be valuable exculpatory evidence, maybe even prove your innocence. They thought you might have spent the evening with this woman, the very night the horrible murder of your wife Laura happened. Has he told you about it?'

Spilwell said nothing.

'By that silence, I'm going to assume that he hasn't. Don't you find that rather strange?'

Jilly had to play this carefully. She couldn't come out and just say certain things. She needed for him to come to his own conclusions.

'Your attorney, he's been a good friend of yours for quite a while, right? If anybody is going to be looking out for your best interests, it's got to be him. You two even hung out together, had dinner in each other's homes, things like that?'

Something seemed to be dawning in Spilwell's eyes. A small light was going on in that darkly smoldering gaze. Somebody close to him, somebody welcome in his city apartment, who could have walked out with, say, a kitchen implement one evening.

'When I found out about this, I knew I needed to come right over and talk to you about it. I thought maybe, *maybe*, you really didn't commit this murder after all.'

'Of course I didn't do it,' he said measuredly, not breaking his gaze. 'I've told you that from day one.'

Jilly, eyebrows raised, put her hands out in exasperation. 'So what I don't understand is, why is your attorney not here behind this? A man who by all rights is willing to go to the mat for you, whatever it takes, especially when your appeal is your very last chance? I'm confused, Doctor, can you help me out here?'

He took the photo from her and stared

at it. Finally he put it down on the table and laid his head in his hands.

'My God,' he murmured, almost too low to hear.

It was the first crack in his cool shell that Jilly had witnessed in over a year. He was catching on. Even a brilliant surgeon can be slow at times, she thought.

'You know, I have to say, I was surprised at how the trial went,' she said. 'Gotta be honest, our track record against Norland Towers isn't all that great. He's smart. He's brutal. I was really ticked off, I figured he'd have you waltzing without breaking a sweat, and I really wanted you for this. I still don't quite get how we nailed a break on this one. The jury didn't do much more than sit down and vote.'

She could tell, point made. The glow in his eyes flared briefly.

She looked at the guard and held up the photo. 'Can I leave this with him?' she asked. The guard approached and inspected it, handed it back with a nod, saying he would deliver it to Spilwell's cell after their meeting.

'If you did not kill Laura,' Jilly said

quietly, bending in close to Spilwell, 'then for God's sake, where were you? Why haven't you told anybody that?'

Spilwell sighed deeply, looked as if he might break. Then the wall descended around him again. He just stared at her without a further word.

Damn this guy, she thought. He's stone cold. Of course everybody thinks he did it.

Jilly stood up. 'The photo is now yours, Doctor. I'm thinking that maybe you need to do some thinking about this.' She carefully placed one of her cards on top of the photo. 'In case you want to give me a call. But in any case, you should definitely consult with your attorney when he next contacts you. Maybe he just overlooked telling you about this. Or maybe . . . it wasn't news to him.'

She told the guard she was ready to leave and looked one last time at Spilwell. He simply stared up at her without a trace of an expression. The Ice King to the very end. But there had to be a heart beating underneath that façade. If not, it would never have come to this.

Driving back to the city, Jilly put her phone on speaker and called Dan. 'How'd it go, partner?'

'A very productive morning. We're getting there. Things are falling into place. I've been checking on the security cameras along the route and there are quite a few.'

'I'll be back soon and we can divvy up the load.'

'I think with any luck we'll be ready to go before Monday morning. The pieces are actually fitting.'

'Let's hope, partner. Let's hope.'

★ ★ ★

They arrived in mid-morning on Monday. As luck would have it, Norland Towers was just coming off the elevator in the lobby of his building as they were entering. And as luck would have it, his wife Mavis was with him. She wasn't dressed in green but in stylish black, but Jilly noted her hair was as striking as in the pictures and yes, she was wearing emeralds. Beautiful and confident. Beloved, perhaps desperately, by two powerful men.

Towers himself, in an expensive dark suit, seemed taken aback as he saw the two detectives approaching.

'Detective Garvey,' he said smoothly. 'I was told you were by the offices the other day. I'm afraid you've returned at an inopportune moment. We have an important engagement. Have you met my wife Mavis?'

'I've never had the pleasure.' Jilly nodded and smiled briefly at Mavis, then turned her attention back to Towers. 'I'm afraid, Mr. Towers, I'm going to have to ask you to come with us. Your engagement is going to have to wait.'

Whatever passed for an icy smile disappeared, replaced by an imperious glower. 'I beg your pardon?'

'Are you coming with us willingly, sir, or do we need to make this an official arrest? We don't really wish to make a scene or anything.'

Towers looked back and forth from Jilly to Dan, who both stood with serious expressions. He quickly surmised that intimidation was not going to work. He turned to Mavis.

'I don't know what this is, dear, but I'll clear it up quickly. Do you mind going on without me?'

For a moment she was taken aback but quickly recovered, smiled graciously, and said, 'Of course.'

She disappeared through the front door of the building before Towers gave the detectives a supremely nasty look and said quietly, 'Whatever this is, you're both going to regret it.'

'We'll see about that,' Jilly smiled brightly. 'This way then?'

* * *

'Would you like an attorney present for this interview?' Jilly asked. They had deliberately selected the least inviting interview room, resplendent with peeling wall paint and the oldest and hardest chairs in the building.

Towers still sat with patrician bearing, as if his ratty metal chair were a throne of a sort. But he was clearly uncomfortable despite himself.

'I *am* an attorney,' he growled. 'As you know.'

Jilly and Dan were on the opposite side of the slate-grey table from him. Dan was half-sitting on the table, leaning in slightly, and Jilly was standing, going through a large manila folder, pulling out various sheets and scanning them.

'Would you happen to know a man named Mark Zanello?' she asked suddenly.

'The name is not ringing a bell with me, Detective. Who is he?'

'So you didn't make a phone call to him on Friday the eighteenth?'

'I cannot say as I remember having done such a thing.'

He was sure they were bluffing. He was sure the evidence didn't exist. He figured they'd check his phone record — if they could get by his legal stonewalling — and find nothing. Smug bastard.

'Were you in town on Friday?'

'Actually, no. I was out of town until late Sunday. I didn't return to my office until Monday morning.'

'And may I ask, where were you?'

'I was at a professional seminar, one hundred miles away. Would you like to check on that? I'll be glad to provide you with references.'

'Thank you. We'll get to them. Did you fly?'

'Actually, I drove. It's a beautiful drive, down the coast. Santa Cristina, you must know it. A lovely beach resort town, perfect for a getaway seminar.'

'You were alone, or did your wife accompany you?'

'No, alas, she had prior commitments and couldn't join me. It would have been quite nice. Although I was insanely busy. You know how those things are.'

'Suppose we were to tell you that there is someone who claims to have met with you in their office on that Saturday morning?'

'I'd say they were mistaken. Or lying.'

'Mr. Towers, the office you maintain in this city, that's not your only one, is it?'

'No. My partner and I practice in several states. Towers and Bridges has satellite offices in New York, Chicago, and Houston.'

Jilly again switched gears.

'Mr. Towers, are you aware that a person named Kerry Moran came to your office with what she believed was evidence that might clear your client Dane Spilwell?'

'Oh yes. I heard about that when I got back. She left some kind of computer file for me. It was nonsense. Just a crank.'

'So you looked at what you call the computer file that she left for you?'

'Very peremptorily. Just enough to see it was a waste of my time. I instructed my assistant to make sure the woman didn't get through again.'

'Had there been any possibility of it being something exculpatory, of course you would have given it serious consideration, given your client's position, what with you preparing an appeal of his murder conviction and all?'

'Of course. What's your point, Detective?'

Dan had still not spoken. He simply sat on the edge of the desk and watched Towers silently. It seemed to be slightly unnerving to Towers.

'So you didn't look at the file until Monday then?'

'That's correct.'

'She dropped it off with your assistant on Friday. And you were not in the city after that until late Sunday?'

'That's correct.'

Jilly played the first card. She extracted four photographic printouts and laid them, one by one, in front of Towers.

'So you're telling me this could not be you, at a pay phone at a convenience store on Webley Avenue, last Friday evening?' She pointed to the date stamps on the pictures.

Towers looked momentarily flustered but he recovered instantly. 'Ridiculous. That is not me. And I don't know that I want to persist in this nonsense any further. Whatever you're suggesting, I don't like it.' He started to rise. 'Am I free to go?'

'No, Mr. Towers, you are not. Please sit back down.' That was Dan, and he said it abruptly enough that Towers did stop and sit back down in surprise.

'As an attorney,' Jilly continued, 'you'd

likely advise your client to stop talking right about now, so suppose you just listen to what we have to say for a little bit.'

She pulled out more sheets and looked them over. 'You drive a late model Lexus, silvery-grey, the official name of the color is Opaline Pearl. You have vanity plates, they read MAG IURIS. I'm told that's a shortening of 'Magister Iuris,' which is Latin for 'Master of Law'.'

She laid two more printout sheets over one of the others.

'You know, it's an interesting thing, nowadays there are *so many* security cameras everywhere. It's pretty much impossible to go several blocks without showing up on one or another of them. This is a blowup from a security camera on a bank ATM four blocks down Webley from the convenience store. You'll note the automobile parked at the curb there. The plate is visible. That's your car, Mister Towers. You'll note the time stamp on this one as well. We've got you at that phone, Mr. Towers.'

She pulled out another sheet. 'Now, the

interesting thing is that Mark Zanello, whom you say you never met and don't know, received a phone call from that very phone at that very time.'

Towers began to say something but thought better of it. He was beginning to act as lawyer and client in one, seeing the situation was much more perilous than he had originally thought.

'Going back to that photograph of you at the phone,' Jilly said, fishing one of the photos out and holding it up, 'that's a very nice tie you're wearing in that picture. Very distinctive, not just the tie but that stickpin.' She pulled out still another photograph, this one a blowup from a slick magazine. 'Suspiciously resembles the tie and pin you wore a couple of months back when you held a press conference during your client Dane Spilwell's trial. Rather sloppy of you. Frankly, I'm disappointed. Now, you say you didn't know Mark Zanello. I assume you have no idea who Mort Blessing is either?'

'No, I do not,' Towers spat.

'He's better known to his friends as

Satch. He's a waiter. Well, that's what you'd call his day job. He's actually a musician. He just left town this week. He received an irresistible offer to play in Chicago.'

Towers said nothing. Jilly looked at Dan. 'Seems Detective Lee, here, dug up some fascinating information about that.'

'I located Mr. Blessing in Chicago,' Dan said. 'It turns out he took his cell phone with him and once I obtained that number, it was easy enough to contact him. He told me he had received an offer to front a jazz band with some mind bogglingly high-end gigs. A jazz combo. Television, radio, live concerts. Go figure.'

Now it was Dan's turn to dig through his own file and pull out a sheet.

'It was an odd offer. He had to accept it on the spot and leave town that night. It came from a booking agent and promoter named Len Garfield.' Dan looked up and down the paper he held. 'Quite a colorful gent, this Len Garfield guy. The Chicago police know him well. A few racketeering charges and some rather serious stuff.' Dan looked up. 'He spent a little time behind bars, but was acquitted of most of those charges. Perhaps you're familiar with Mr. Garfield, considering you were his attorney on many of those cases?'

'I am not going to listen to any more of this idiocy,' Towers said. 'I'm not under arrest, I'm leaving.'

Jilly sighed. 'Okay. Then I guess that's that.'

Towers stood up and straightened his tie. 'I'm going to go.'

'No, Mr. Towers. We are going to place you under arrest.' She pulled out her Miranda Rights card and began to recite. 'You have the right to remain silent . . . '

Dan had the handcuffs at the ready and snapped them on his wrists in front of him. Now, she thought, maybe we get his attention.

Jilly finished the recitation and waited for the answer to 'Do you understand each of these rights I have explained to you?' Then she proceeded. 'Now then. Do you want to talk, or do you want to keep listening? Please sit back down, Mr. Towers.'

He eased back into the chair and coolly

eyed them without saying a word.

'Let me tell you what we think happened. We may revise our overview as we fill it in with new evidence, but be assured, we *will* fill it in, with good solid work. My partner and I are good at that. You may or may not have actually driven down the coast, but you were in your office on Friday evening. You found the computer file to which you referred, and were possibly intrigued by whatever note your assistant Ms. Grymes left with it. You didn't just give it a cursory look, you explored it carefully. And it disturbed you. Just why, well, let's come back to that.

'You were more than disturbed. I'd say you were distraught. You saw the need to take action immediately. Perhaps for whatever reason, you weren't thinking very clearly. In any case, for some reason you decided to start by contacting Mark Zanello. You had his phone number. You called to set up a meeting with him. But you thought it unwise to use your own phone. So you drove to a convenience store that you just *happened* to know had a public phone. Not all that many of those around anymore, are there? You parked three blocks away from the store. A bit of a marginal neighborhood, I'd say. I bet you were concerned about that beautiful Lexus of yours the whole time.

'Mark was on his way out to meet somebody but he must have agreed to meet you, so you drove over to his apartment. We know he was there because he grabbed the mail from his box as he left. We're thinking you had him drive you somewhere quiet to talk. There's a nice little 'pocket park' several blocks from Mark's place. Very quiet side street. Almost no traffic. The park has lots of trees, little gardens, a gated fence around it, used by the neighborhood. There's even a little indented drive-up off the street. Very private. It's usually closed up at night but you were able to get in. The conversation did not go the way you had hoped. You wanted to convince him to get his girlfriend to shut up about what they had seen. What you couldn't have known was that she was no longer his girlfriend, and things were exceedingly bitter between them. Mark was experiencing his own demons. I imagine he wasn't very cooperative. He probably got angry. Maybe physical, I don't know. In any case, being the brilliant strategist, you had a Plan B at the ready. You brought a .38 special with you and shot him twice in the side of the head.'

Towers said nothing but took on an expression as if this was the silliest tale he had ever heard.

'As it happens,' Dan interjected, 'someone in the apartment building next to the park called in to the police that she had heard what might have been shots. Coming from the pocket park.'

'There must have been blood,' Jilly continued. 'We've got crews scouring the park now, looking for traces. No doubt you disposed of the gun. We'll do our best to find it, just like you did your best to get him out of the park and into the drive-up on the dark, quiet street. Into his trunk. Drive him somewhere you think he won't be found, and when he is, it'll look like a gang shooting.'

Dan pulled out another sheet. 'Abandoned buildings on Pilsen. Interestingly, the former owner of a few of them recently copped a plea on several charges of arson and insurance fraud. He was represented in his pleas by one Stillman Morris, who is an associate partner with . . . Towers and Bridges. Now what are the odds?'

'Pretty good plan, in fact,' Jilly resumed. 'You knew nobody was likely to go anywhere near that building for months. Maybe years. What you didn't figure on was a homeless couple ingenious enough to get into the building.'

'You helped,' Dan added. 'You didn't bother to nail the door back up again. You figured if the door lock snapped, it would be good enough. That was a little sloppy, don't you think?'

Jilly shrugged and looked at Dan. 'Well, it's not like Mr. Towers hangs out with the kind of people who frequent that neighborhood. How was he to know?' She turned back to Towers.

'I like this next set of moves, these were pretty slick and imaginative. But you are, after all, a criminal lawyer, as you reminded us. You undoubtedly wore gloves throughout all of this, left no fingerprints. You took Mark's valuables — his wallet, watch, and phone. You left the wallet and watch under the seat of his car. You left his phone on the seat where it could be picked up by anybody exploring the car. And drove Mark's car a few blocks away, still in a very sketchy area, and left it open with the keys in it, figuring it would be stolen and all sorts of interesting things could happen to throw us off your trail. We might be sent racing to the four winds before all was done. Nice.'

She tilted her head. 'You may have been congratulating yourself on handling a bad situation so well, but you must have started to come down from your adrenaline high by now and realized that this was not the way to handle the situation. You couldn't go around knocking off all the other principals in this little play. It was messy. Your visibility increased, the danger grew with every moment. You had to get more subtle. So you summoned your investigator the next day and had him ply a scheme on Kerry Moran. In the meantime you contacted your friend Len in Chicago and had him tender Satch an offer he couldn't refuse. You got rid of Satch, Mark was not going to be talking to anyone, and you figured Kerry would be motivated to give up. And then, maybe you really *did* drive back down to Santa Cristina on Saturday, where you could make a point of being seen.'

'Now the question is,' Dan chimed in, 'just *why* was all this so crucial to you to silence these people and suppress this when you just told us it was inconsequential and meaningless evidence?'

'Well, he might argue it could actually harm Dr. Spilwell's appeal case,' offered Jilly. 'After all, Mr. Towers has been a close and valued friend of Dr. Spilwell's for many years now. He no doubt feels terrible since he booted the doctor's case so badly.'

'Good point,' Dan replied. 'I certainly would. What a remarkable upset.'

'A true debacle,' Jilly agreed, nodding, lips pursed. 'And what with how the two of them spent so much social time together, in each other's homes, with each other's families . . . '

'Sharing so much,' Dan said.

'Perhaps even lending and borrowing back and forth,' Jilly said. She noted Towers' expression was growing darker. She turned back to him. 'Perhaps you borrowed one of Dr. Spilwell's kitchen implements, for example, but then you turned around and lost it? Which leads us to another interesting little detail . . . you know, Mr. Towers, there's someone else who used that very same pay phone at that convenience store a while back. Are you familiar with what I'm talking about?'

Towers said nothing, just glowered darker and darker.

'The very last person to call Laura Spilwell before she died. How about that for a coincidence? Laura's friends in her book club said she called to say she'd be delayed. She had been detoured by a call by someone she must have known and trusted, perhaps an invitation to stop at a restaurant she liked for a mysterious impromptu conversation over a drink. That detour took her past the alley where she was stabbed to death. By a killer who also attempted to fabricate a fiction about a robbery gone bad.' Jilly shrugged. 'We find this fascinating, don't you?

'So the point of all this,' continued Jilly, pulling still another photo out of her folder and dropping it on the table in front of Towers, 'is just *why?* Why the desperate and *very* risky attempt at a cover-up? And why the death of Laura Spilwell to begin with?'

The picture on the table was Kerry's shot of Spilwell and the back of the mystery woman in red hair and emeralds.

'You knew,' Jilly said. 'You knew Dr. Spilwell and your wife were having an affair.'

Towers made a noise deep in his throat. 'Shut the hell up.'

'Not just a fling, a very passionate affair. Spilwell loved her. He was going to divorce his wife. Likely Mavis was going to do the same with you!'

'No!' Towers shouted, jumping up. 'No! Never! It would never have come to that!'

His eyes glowed with sheer hate at the two of them.

'Spilwell thought you didn't know,' Jilly said. 'He was never going to let it get out. He cared too much for Mavis. He didn't want to hurt her. He was afraid of what you might do. He never suspected you knew, did he?'

'Stupid fool,' Towers muttered. He grew quiet and sat back down.

'How did you find out, anyway? Someone earlier this week told me that they thought women always knew about cheating spouses, but that men tended to not even have a clue. But you knew. You picked up on the subtle clues, didn't you? You might have made a good detective, Mr. Towers. You notice details. You figured it all out. Mavis was cheating on you, and with your good friend Dane Spilwell. That had to really eat at you.'

Towers sunk his head deep into his hands, making the cuffs clink, and all of a sudden began to laugh. It grew louder and more bizarre. The silence that abruptly followed was even stranger.

'Oh, what the hell,' he suddenly said,

lifting his head and sitting back.

'It doesn't matter,' he said with a serene smile. 'I'll never serve a single day.' He just kept staring and smiling at them, a cat who had just consumed not one but several canaries.

'Just what do you mean?' Jilly asked.

'Detective, I was indeed in Santa Cristina that weekend. And yes, there was a conference at which I was registered. But it was a cover. I've been back and forth to Santa Cristina a few times the past couple of weeks, even back and forth this past weekend.'

'More privileged duplicity, Mr. Towers? Don't tell me you've been carrying on an affair as well!'

He shook his head in amusement. 'You are nowhere near as smart as you think. No, I wish it were something that . . . pedestrian. There's an excellent clinic in Santa Cristina. The Treadwell Clinic. Perhaps you've heard of it.'

'Cancer,' said Dan. 'You've got cancer.'

Towers' eyes bulged open in mocking awe. 'Very good, Detective Lee. Would you like to tell me what *kind* of cancer?'

There was no reply.

'Pancreatic cancer, Detective. A very virulent case. Do you know much about that particular little devil?'

'It's basically a death sentence,' Jilly said somberly. 'How long, Mr. Towers?'

'A matter of weeks if I'm lucky. I'm told it's very, very fast.'

'When did you find out?'

'Less than a fortnight ago. You do know the term 'fortnight'? Pity it's fallen out of use.'

'So you've known for under two weeks. Just before the verdict came down.'

'That's when the first pain began, yes.' There was an awkward silence. 'It doesn't really matter. My legal team will keep this hung up for as long as it takes. Then, well . . . then I won't be around.'

'And your wife? Does Mavis know? About the cancer, I mean.'

'Of course she knows.'

'But not about your murders, I presume. Or that you knew about her and Spilwell.'

Towers said nothing.

'You were willing to kill the wife of one

of your best friends.'

He snorted. 'Some friend. Plotting to steal my wife.'

'And you would send him to prison for life for something he didn't do.'

'In return for something he *did* do, that he'd never be called to account for. A despicable traitor. He got off easily. He deserved far worse. It was diabolically ingenious of me, don't you think?'

'You killed another innocent young man. For what?'

Towers shrugged. His voice had turned low and dark but stayed very calm. It was as if some switch had been turned inside of him; Jilly found it unnerving.

'Necessity. What's the expression the government likes to use? Collateral damages? Acceptable losses?'

'And you likely destroyed the life of still another person that you don't even know. She probably feels she might as well be dead.' Jilly bent down, leaning on the table, and stared into his eyes. Nothing but unrepentant coldness and death stared back. 'None of this means anything to you, does it?'

Towers shrugged. 'You know, you got the story pretty close. Not perfect. A few minor details are off. But better, far better than I would have given you credit for.'

'So the only thing that seems to matter to you, Mr Towers, is . . . what? Winning? Your ego? You're not going to tell me you actually love Mavis. What I'm looking at right now, I don't see much love and tenderness there.'

'Shows just what you know, Detective.' He had a way of making the term 'Detective' sound like a contemptuous slur. 'In fact Mavis is what I love above everything and anything else in this world.'

'But to have her stolen from you,' Dan interjected. 'To *lose* her. You'd never allow to happen, right?'

Towers turned his gaze to Dan, narrowing his eyes. 'Never. Nobody beats me.'

'We beat you in the Spilwell case. But then, you threw that one, didn't you?'

Towers just tilted his head with a tight smile.

Jilly couldn't help herself. 'I'd like to

know something, Mr. Towers. You made some pretty stupid mistakes here. Here we all thought you were so brilliant and all. Did you want us to catch you, once you knew your days were limited? Or did the news upset you so much that you got sloppy?'

Another deep glare. For a moment he appeared to begin to say something, but thought better of it. He said, with sarcasm, 'Perhaps it's the level of pain. Are you familiar with cancer, Detective? There are things that distract even the most single-minded.'

*　*　*

They sat at a table in the police station cafeteria — it was really little more than a dispensary for coffee and other drinks — neither really wanting to say a word. Jilly stirred her tea and Dan contemplated his cup of coffee. They stayed that way for what seemed a very long time.

'The man's a monster,' Jilly finally said quietly, not looking up.

'You told me that Reggie once said that

murder was the ultimate act of narcissism, right? He's the ultimate narcissist.'

'He's going to beat it too.'

'I wouldn't say a death sentence from fast-moving cancer is exactly beating it,' Dan observed.

'He'll never serve a day in jail. He was right. He'll keep it knotted up right to the end.'

'He can't be happy about what kind of hit his reputation is going to take. Not to mention Mavis will be gone as fast as she can clear out. He may never see her again.'

'He'll still find a way to see this as a win,' Jilly muttered.

'For once,' said Dan, 'I'm rooting for the cancer.'

10

To Jilly, it seemed that everything moved at light speed from that point on. Before the end of that Monday, Dane Spilwell had fired Norland Towers and retained another high-powered attorney, who immediately announced that new developments in the case 'would exonerate Dr. Spilwell and necessitate an expeditious reversal of his guilty verdict.' Clearly Spilwell had decided that he needed to tell the whole story, and he did, publicly and in shocking detail. It dovetailed with the Police Department's announcement that the Laura Spilwell case had been reopened and that Norland Towers was being charged in her murder as well as in that of Mark Zanello.

The various news media sought out Mavis Towers to interview her, but she was ahead of them. She had already left her husband and seemingly dropped off the face of the earth. She would never appear in the public eye again.

Norland Towers' cancer accelerated with a vengeance, almost as if he were goading it to move ever more rapidly. He was hospitalized within another two weeks and placed in a hospice shortly thereafter. He would die less than a month after his arrest. He never saw the inside of a jail or prison.

It was reported that not a single person, except for medical personnel, had ever been observed at his bedside.

Jilly attempted a few phone calls to Kerry Moran over the following weeks. Her depression seemed to darken steadily for a while but she was finally beginning to once again put her life together. One day they agreed to meet briefly in Sunset Park, not far from where Kerry had met Earl Ryan.

Kerry was already on the bench, holding a cup of hot coffee in her hands, staring blankly ahead of her, looking pale and thin. She looked up when Jilly approached. She actually smiled, though it seemed weak and belabored.

'How are things?' Jilly asked.

Kerry shrugged. 'Okay, I guess. I haven't been drinking in two whole days now. I'd forgotten what it felt like to not have a hangover.'

'You have to move on, Kerry.'

'I know. But how? I killed everything around me. I destroyed my relationship with Mark. I destroyed him emotionally, and then I destroyed him for real. And I screwed up my whole life as well.'

'You didn't mean for any of that to happen. I know that's not much help. You still made mistakes, and yes, you will have to contend with the consequences of them. Some pretty serious ones. Take it one day at a time.'

'You know what's funny?' Kerry said. 'I got a call from a big advertising agency. I mean, like a multinational. They said they want to talk to me about a position. I can't be sure but somehow I think Dr. Spilwell had something to do with that.'

'I wasn't sure whether he'd be grateful to you or not. He damned well should be. But I wasn't sure. Maybe he is behind this. I hope you're going to go talk to them.'

'I said I needed a little bit of time to get myself together, but yeah, I think I will.'

Jilly nodded. 'Good. Don't wait too long.'

'Funny, they told me that was how Mark got his spirit back. He stopped his downward plunge and threw himself into his work. Maybe I'll find that works for me, too.'

'Be patient. You'll come out of this.'

Kerry turned to look at Jilly and her eyes were moist. 'You've been so nice to me these past few weeks. By all rights you shouldn't be able to stand me. I've been nothing but trouble for you.'

Jilly had to laugh, which surprised Kerry. 'Yes, you were. You were the biggest pain in the behind I've had in some time. But at heart I know you're a good person, Kerry, and I guess I just decided you needed a break.' Her gaze turned faraway as she thought of earlier times. 'My old partner, his name was Reggie Martinez. He once told me that most of the people we encountered in our job were lost causes. By the time we got to them, they were beyond any help we had to give them.'

'That's pretty cynical,' Kerry sniffed.

'But the funny thing was, underneath that tough surface, Reggie wasn't really all that much a cynic. There was more to that thought. He would finish it by saying that it was that much more important that we do what we could to salvage the ones that still had hope.' Jilly started to stand up, putting a hand on Kerry's shoulder. 'You're savable. Think of yourself that way.'

She still didn't really like this crazy young woman, but she did feel sympathy for her. She hoped before it was all over that she'd find some peace. And maybe grow up in the process. Staying in motion, that was the answer, she was convinced. Just as she had to move on from her memories of Reggie.

Don't look back.

Stravinsky on her phone interrupted her reverie. She decided she'd need to change that ringtone, find something more appropriate.

'Jilly, it's Dan. We got a new one.'

'Tell me where, partner, I'm on my way.'

She took the info, said her final goodbye to Kerry and headed out. It was time to change gears and move on.

We do hope that you have enjoyed reading this large print book.

Did you know that all of our titles are available for purchase?

We publish a wide range of high quality large print books including:
Romances, Mysteries, Classics
General Fiction
Non Fiction and Westerns

Special interest titles available in large print are:
The Little Oxford Dictionary
Music Book, Song Book
Hymn Book, Service Book

Also available from us courtesy of Oxford University Press:
Young Readers' Dictionary
(large print edition)
Young Readers' Thesaurus
(large print edition)

For further information or a free brochure, please contact us at:
Ulverscroft Large Print Books Ltd.,
The Green, Bradgate Road, Anstey,
Leicester, LE7 7FU, England.
Tel: (00 44) **0116 236 4325**
Fax: (00 44) **0116 234 0205**

THE GALLOWS IN MY GARDEN

Richard Deming

Grace Lawson and her brother Donald stand to inherit their late father's millions when they reach the age of twenty-one — but someone in their household of family, servants and regular guests seems intent on ensuring they don't live that long. Donald disappears, and a would-be killer dogs Grace's every move. Not wanting to involve the police and create a family scandal, Grace turns to private investigator Manville Moon — who is unaware of how complex the case will be, or that his own life will be threatened . . .

IT'S HER FAULT

Tony Gleeson

An aging university professor insists to Detective Frank Vandegraf that his estranged wife is trying to kill him, but the problem is that she's nowhere to be found. A relative claims that it's the other way around: the husband is actually threatening to kill his wife. When the professor turns up murdered shortly thereafter, with a mysterious note lying on his chest that says 'IT'S HER FAULT', Frank redoubles his efforts to locate the missing wife, his prime suspect. But when he does, the case becomes even more baffling . . .

THE BESSIE BLUE KILLER

Richard A. Lupoff

A film studio sets out to create a documentary about the Tuskegee Airmen, a unit of African-Americans who flew combat missions in World War Two — but filming has barely begun when a corpse is found on the set. Hobart Lindsey, insurance investigator turned detective, enters the scene, aided by Marvia Plum, his policewoman girlfriend. Soon he uncovers a mystery stretching half a century into the past — and suddenly and unexpectedly is flying through a hazardous murder investigation by the seat of his pants!

UNHOLY GROUND

Catriona McCuaig

When midwife Maudie Rouse marries the love of her life, policeman Dick Bryant, the pair could not be happier as they settle into contented domesticity in the village of Llandyfan. But troubles abound for the newlyweds — an abandoned baby, a difficult new district nurse, and the possibility of losing their home — and Maudie must find a way to deal with the problems, in addition to bicycling around the village performing her professional duties. Meanwhile, a grim discovery is made in a local farmer's field . . .